PATH TO CONFESSION

A NOVEL

BY
PAT JACKSON

Pat Jackson

OTHER BOOKS BY PAT JACKSON:

JUDGING ANNA

2020

ISBN: 9798649897549

To Lee

who walks beside me,
patiently and lovingly,
guiding my journey along life's path

Chapter 1

Standing on tiptoe, she carefully glided her hand along the top shelf of the high laundry room cabinet, seeking the item carefully placed there years before. When her fingers finally brushed against something solid, she grasped tightly and gave a tug, pulling from its hiding place the old cloth bag that had lain untouched and almost forgotten for so long. For a moment, her gaze rested on its faded colors and the draw string, still securely tied even after all this time. Her thoughts went back to the day she'd placed it there.

Her husband, who'd had absolutely no interest in its contents, had shaken his head dismissively when consulted about its future, offering no suggestions, and leaving her at a loss as what to do. Thoughts of donating it to the local museum had passed through her mind, but being unwilling to relinquish ownership of something that held such a special place in her heart dictated her decision to keep it, even though there was really no reason to do so. After much consideration, the hard-to-reach laundry room shelf, which was not a practical location for often used items, seemed to offer the best solution for a safe and somewhat secret place for its storage.

With unsteady hands, she forced herself to concentrate on undoing the knotted draw string to quell her sudden emotion. The enormity of the task she was about to embark on almost overwhelmed her. Once the bag was no longer secured, she pulled out the .45 caliber Smith and Wesson revolver, cradling it reverently in her hands.

Precious memories of her father came rushing back as she gazed at the gun. Although he had been dead for many years, his voice echoed plainly in her mind, proudly proclaiming how he'd worn it around his neck when he was a pilot stationed in the Philippines during World War II. Tracing the handle with her fingers brought a smile to her face. Recalling the many times the two of them had taken this very weapon to the firing range suddenly erased all the years he'd been gone. Adamant that she become proficient at handling guns, under his patient tutoring, she'd learned to load, aim, fire, and clean a weapon as well as any man. The owner of the range was impressed by her father's insistence that she become adept at handling a weapon. He remarked several times how more fathers needed to equip their daughters with the knowledge and skill she was learning. It became a ritual that the three of them would spend some time together sharing a drink when she and her dad finished target practice. No lesson was complete until his exhortation about safety issues, plus the importance of proper weapon care had been delivered. Without fail on the ride home, he'd review how the morning session had gone, ending with a lecture on the merits of knowing self-protection strategies. Holding the revolver he loved so much and recalling those conversations made her feel close to him.

A unique individual, holding himself and those he cared about to a code of impeccable conduct and unfailing loyalty, there had been a bond between them unlike any other she'd experienced. He was not really a harsh man, but he had been demanding in his expectations and unrelenting when they were not met. His standards included keeping commitments and protecting those he loved with unparalleled fierceness. There was no doubt that he would not have a problem with what she was about to do; she was confident of that.

Removing the six bullets from the bag, she remembered how he'd emphasized over and over that weapons must be stored with appropriate ammunition. As the bullets clicked into the cylinder, she noted the revolver's pristine condition. That was another thing her father had also been explicit about; no weapon was to be put away until it was properly cleaned. "Dirty weapons and those without ammunition are of no value," he'd told her over and over.

When the last bullet was in place and the safety fully engaged, she picked up the large quilted handbag lying on the counter beneath the cabinet. Carefully she placed the loaded gun in the bottom of it and then added the tightly closed cellophane package, a pair of canvas pull-on shoes, some gloves, and a large rolled cloth tote bag she'd carefully assembled earlier. Placing her wallet, glasses, checkbook, tissues, make-up bag and make-up remover cloths over the other items completed her task. After briskly snapping the bag's fastener closed, with an air of determination, she walked quickly to the garage and got in her modest sedan, ready to begin the journey that had consumed her thoughts for months.

Chapter 2

The drive to her destination was uneventful. She pulled into the crowded shopping center parking lot and drove slowly, looking for a parking space in view of the surveillance camera that swept the entire area. Her efforts were soon rewarded as a car backed out of a spot directly across from it. After carefully parking, she exited, locked her vehicle, and made her way to the entrance of the large department store bearing the name Grafton's across its roof. At the door, she paused, making sure she was in range of the store's security camera, removed her sunglasses and put them in her purse before pulling the handle of the heavy glass door. A large smile adorned her face as she cheerfully greeted the two associates standing at the cash registers.

"Good morning, how are you ladies today?" she said to engage them in conversation. "I bet it is going to be a busy day for you with this huge sale going on."

The women smiled and agreed. They chatted briefly as she selected a shopping cart. She asked about the "early bird specials" and mentioned how she always looked forward to their annual sales.

"We have some really good bargains today. Take your time," one of them advised, adding, "you don't want to miss anything."

"Well I really shouldn't even be here; I have a party at my house this evening, but I just couldn't resist coming. I hope I can find everything I need and get back home in time to get ready for it," was her laughing reply. As she headed toward the boutique section of the store, all three women chuckled.

The beginning-of-summer sale was in full swing; customers milled throughout the aisles looking at all the displays. Without paying too much attention, she selected a couple of tops, a pair of pants and a skirt, placing them in the cart before meandering to the back of the store where a second set of fitting rooms was located. Pretending to browse, she watched carefully until the salesclerk came out of the area with a load of items to be returned to stock. When the clerk's back was to her, she hurried into the last stall, stopping just long enough to get one of the 'hold' tickets provided for customers wanting to have items reserved for them. Once she securely latched the door, she removed the red ankle-length, crinkled skirt and three-quarter sleeved checkered blouse, leaving her dressed in black tights covered by a knee-length white t-shirt. The black canvas shoes with tissue paper stuffed down tight in the toes to make their bigger size fit her feet were also pulled from her purse. Just as she'd practiced so many times, she wiggled her feet into them almost effortlessly. A short, black, curly wig emerged from the cellophane bag and she pulled it over her blond hair with practiced care. Applying a bright pink lipstick to her lips and re-shaping her eyebrows with a dark eyebrow pencil completed her transformation. Scrutinizing her new look, she was satisfied with the results. After placing her sandals in the bottom of the unrolled tote bag and putting the makeup inside the purse, she wrapped the skirt and blouse she'd been wearing around the purse and carefully positioned the bundle on top of them. Cocking an ear to the fitting room door convinced her no one was in the immediate area. Scribbling her name on the 'hold' ticket taken earlier, she slipped it over the items she'd placed in the shopping cart and made her way toward the fitting room area exit, stopping just long enough to hang them on the rod provided for garments being held for customers. A quick glance only revealed browsing customers whose interest was focused on the merchandise displays. Casually, she sauntered out of the area, carefully making her way to the front of the store.

No one paid any attention to her as she moved through the shoppers. The store was very crowded; many people were coming and going. It wasn't long before a group of teenagers began making their way to the exit. Keeping her head down and averting her face from the camera, she moved closer to them, pretending to be part of their crowd as they left the store. Once outside and away from the camera, she walked quickly down the sidewalk toward the bus stop at the very end of the parking lot.

Chapter 3

In less than two minutes, she was on the bus. Having taken the trip on three separate occasions, she knew the trip to her next destination, the city's popular recreational lake park would take between 30 and 40 minutes, depending on the number of stops the bus made to take on other travelers. Sure enough, thirty-three minutes later, she was off the bus. To any casual observer, she was just part of the crowd enjoying a fun day, walking casually down the path, past shops and eating places, making her way toward one of the lake-side establishments. As the sign "Welcome to Taking It Easy," came into view, she inhaled. Its installation had been such a special day in her life. As she read the message below it, "a place you can rent boats and paddle boards and purchase everything you need for a relaxing adventure," thoughts of her past life flashed through her mind. Taking in the long pier positioned at the end of the lake with several boats docked along it, for a moment her eyes misted with tears. Giving her head a determined shake, her focus moved to the large sporting goods store adjoining the pier. It looked the same; no indication of the controversy that had surrounded it for months was evident. Not knowing how long it would be until the opportunity she needed would present itself, patiently she leaned on the lakeside rail, pretending to be enthralled by the gently lapping water. Several minutes elapsed before a group of young men passed her and made their way to the boats, obviously intent on renting one. Following a brief conversation, they approached a man wearing a Taking-It-Easy cap. After a brief discussion which she couldn't hear, the group headed toward the entrance of the store. Moving quickly, she began walking close behind them, strategically positioning herself so that anyone looking would assume she was part of the jolly entourage. They paid her no attention as they laughed and joked together. She was close enough so that the guy holding the door open for the group waited until she entered before he, too, stepped into the store. She paused just inside the building at a counter display of sunscreen, feigning interest in the products.

The man wearing the Taking-It-Easy cap motioned for them to follow him to a long counter along the side wall as their discussion regarding a boat rental continued. Continuing her charade of selecting a sunscreen, she waited, watching them out of the corner of her eye, until their attention was completed diverted. When they were deep in conversation, unnoticed, she quickly moved to a nearby aisle, and ducked behind a display of paddle boards, completely hidden from the group at the counter. From her secluded spot, it was easy to survey the layout of the building.

Although it had been quite a while since her last visit, her memory of it was correct. It was a relief to see that no changes had been made; it was exactly the same, including the stock room along the back wall marked 'Employee's Only.' The man helping the students also looked the same and there was no reason to think his habits had changed. She knew most of his activity surrounding the business happened at the pier, with customers inspecting the boats and paddle boards and discussing rentals. Only one employee worked inside the store, but on Fridays that person did not come in until after lunch. The man, who was supposed to cover store activities in her absence, rarely stayed inside the building. The occasional shopper had to pass him, and the entrance door had an alarm announcing when anyone came into the store, alerting a customer had arrived. All rental arrangements were conducted at the register inside the store. Once she'd confirmed that other than the guys at the counter and herself, no one else was inside the store, she carefully maneuvered her hands into the gloves she'd included in the tote bag. After a few minutes, the rental agreement concluded, the man handed a boat key to one of the guys. He followed them to the door and watched as they headed out for their adventure on the lake. As he stood looking at them through the glass, noiselessly she stepped to the center of the aisle and waited.

When he finally turned from the door and saw her, a look of surprise crossed his face. His tone friendly, he said, "Hello, I didn't know anyone was here. Can I help you?"

Without a word, she pulled the revolver from her purse, cocked it, aimed, and fired. The sound of the shot was ear-splitting. The bullet hit him squarely in the chest. Without hesitating, she pulled the trigger again, watching as his expression faded into nothingness when the second bullet struck just below where the first one had hit. Wordlessly, he fell to the floor. Thrusting the gun back into her purse and quickly surveying the store's premises to be sure no one had entered during the confrontation, she did not look at the figure lying on the floor. Satisfied no one else was on the premises, she hurried to the stock room. With a quick push of her sleeved elbow, she easily opened the exit door located in the center of its back wall. She stepped out of the building, pausing just long enough to hear the decisive click signaling the door closed behind her.

Huge dumpsters sat on either side of the door, about a foot or so off the paved driveway that intersected with a street just past the end of the building. Once again performing a quick survey to confirm there was no one to witness her presence, she quickly pulled the gloves from her hands and shoved them into the canvas bag. Cautiously making her way down the driveway, being sure to stay on the pavement so as not to leave any footprints in the dirt, in less than a minute she was back on the winding path beside the lake. A lack of any unusual activity led her to believe that the sound of the gunshots hadn't attracted any attention; people still wandered about watching the ducks on the lake, eating ice cream, and enjoying the afternoon. Nonchalantly, she headed toward the bus stop at a leisurely pace, arriving just as a bus pulled up to the curb. She boarded, dropped her coins in the slot and sat down on the first available seat, just part of the crowd.

Chapter 4

Thirty minutes later, when the bus pulled up to the same stop she'd used earlier for boarding, she, along with several other riders, exited. Holding the tote bag close to her side as she nonchalantly strolled toward the department store, she thought about the deed she'd just committed. Strangely calm, she had no remorse for her actions; her only feeling was one of finality. At long last, all connection to her marriage had been severed. She could finally move forward. Relief flooded through her.

Once inside the department store, she grabbed a shopping cart and made her way through the crowd. After snagging a random outfit from the first rack of sale items, once again she made her way to the fitting rooms in the back and entered the first vacant stall, securely latching the door.

Inside the fitting room, she worked quickly. She pulled wig off; using several of the disposable make-up remover cloths, she erased the bright red lipstick and dark eyebrows. Restoring her lips and eyebrows to their normal color, she applied fresh lipstick and eye make-up. From the tote bag, she retrieved the long skirt and blouse and pulled them on over the tights and t-shirt. Her sandals replaced the big tissue-stuffed flats. Running a brush through her long blond hair completed the restoration. She placed the revolver, flats, and wig on the bottom of the designer purse, rerolled the tote bag and laid across on top, followed by her wallet, checkbook, make-up, and pouch containing the used removal cloths. With everything stored appropriately, she paused and inhaled deeply to calm herself, and mentally reviewed the next steps of her well-thought-out plan. As she'd done earlier, she pressed her ear to the door to be sure the immediate area was isolated. When silence confirmed no one was about, she pulled the door open. Stopping to place the outfit she'd just brought into the fitting room on the merchandise return rod and retrieving the items with her name on them from the 'hold' section and placing them in the cart, she headed toward the home section of the store, just another customer looking for sale bargains. A set of candle sticks and some pillowcases joined the clothing items in the cart before she snagged a handbag and a necklace from the accessories section. She made her way to the check-out lanes making sure to choose the line being serviced by one of the clerks she'd exchanged conversation with earlier.

When it was her turn to be checked out, she joked as she placed the items on the counter, "Well, here I am. I think I've seen every item in every department of the store and tried on every outfit."

The clerk smiled. "It sure looks like you've been busy. I'm glad you found some bargains. I hope you had a good time."

"I've certainly been here long enough, haven't I?" she said as she handed over her credit card.

"You got some really good things, Ms. Arnold," the clerk said as she bagged the items. The purchase complete, she thanked the salesclerk and said, "See you next time," before going out the door. In no time Jana was back in her vehicle, headed home.

Jana punched the automatic opener button as she approached her driveway, grateful to see the wide double door rise, enabling her to drive straight into the garage without hesitating. After carefully stopping the car next to three bags of potting soil, one which was opened, she reached into the purse and retrieved the revolver from the bottom of it. Holding it tightly, she stepped out onto the concrete garage floor. Without hesitating, she shoved the gun down into the thick mixture of the open bag. After taking a moment to be sure it was completely obliterated, she rinsed her hands in the garage utility sink before grabbing her purchases from the back seat, and then hurried into the house to continue the tasks on her detailed 'to do' list.

Chapter 5

Her heart pounded as she walked upstairs. The actions she was about to take had been rehearsed in her mind many times but that didn't stop her anxiety. Guided by the carefully thought-out plan she'd devised during the previous months, she spread a sheet from the linen closet on the bottom of the bathtub and placed a large open plastic garbage bag and on top of it. For the second time since putting them on that morning, she removed the long skirt and blouse and stripped off the tights. Not bothering to put on another outfit, she perched on the edge of the bathtub in her underwear reaching for the sewing scissors she'd had sharpened professionally the week before. She set about her task methodically; t-shirt and tights were cut into pieces first, taking special care that every piece fell into the open garbage bag. Next, holding the wig down inside the bag, she whacked it into particles. Likewise, the shredded gloves and tote along with the canvas shoes she'd worn went into it. The lipstick and eyebrow pencil were thrown in, too. After a vigorous shake to compress the contents as much as possible, she tied the bag securely. She tossed the sheet into the laundry hamper and rinsed the tub to be sure no traces of the articles remained. After scanning the area to be sure she'd done everything according to plan, she quickly dressed and made her way to the backyard, garbage bag in hand.

Earlier she'd taken pieces of wood from the big pile next to the fire pit at the end of the patio and positioned them in the bottom of it. She placed the tied bag on top of the wood, added more sticks, and with careful scrutiny confirmed the bag was completely covered. She doused gasoline from the lawn mower gas can over the entire pile.

Reentering the house and going straight to the telephone, she prepared herself to make the call needed to continue her plan. "Be calm," she mumbled as she dialed the number. "Be yourself; don't appear anxious." Her friend answered on the second ring. "Shirley, I'm just checking in with you about tonight," she said brightly. "I have everything, including the S'mores ingredients." She listened as her friend ticked off the list of things she was bringing and then asked the question that was the real purpose of her call.

"What do you think about having the fire burned down to embers before the kids get here? You know those boys can get pretty rambunctious. I hate to have a full fire blazing when they are trying to roast marshmallows. I thought I'd go ahead and light it and let it burn down; what do you think?"

Her friend agreed, just as she'd hoped she would. They talked for a few more minutes ending the call with "see you soon." Jana sighed as she hung up the phone, thankful that the plan was working.

Turning her attention to the upcoming event, she busied herself with food preparation and arranging the buffet bar. At 4:00, she took a long shower, and then, reminding herself how important appearances might be, dressed for the evening choosing jeans and a beautifully embroidered tunic top as the outfit she would wear. She took special care applying make-up and styling her hair, finishing by spraying her favorite cologne on her neck and wrists. By 5:15, she was ready for the party. It was on purpose that the television remained off; there was no reason to see any news alerts.

At 5:30, she went out to the fire pit. Checking from every angle she made sure the wood still covered the filled garbage bag she'd placed there earlier. When the lit match fell onto the gasoline-soaked sticks, a huge blaze erupted, its flames dancing toward the sky. Waiting for it to die down a bit, a quick review of the events of the day played through her mind. Confident everything had gone according to plan, a sigh of relief escaped her. By 6:45, nothing but glowing embers remained in the pit. It was perfect for roasting marshmallows.

Chapter 6

Shirley and her husband arrived promptly at 7:00. She and Jana had been best friends for many years and as soon as she saw her, Jana could read the apprehension in friend's eyes, confirming she knew what had happened.

"Hey girl, are you ready for this shindig?" she asked in a carefree tone, bracing herself to respond to the news her friend might tell her.

"Jana, you haven't heard anything, have you?" Shirley asked.

Acutely aware of the intenseness of her friend's gaze, Jana tilted her head and raised her eyebrow in a puzzled manner before she asked, "What are you talking about?"

Taking a deep breath, Shirley stated, "James died this afternoon."

"James died?" Jana gasped. "Oh, my goodness! What happened?" Putting her hand over her chest to feign surprise, she asked, "Was he in a car accident? How did you find out?"

"No, it wasn't a car accident. He was murdered at Taking It Easy," her friend said quietly. "It flashed across the TV screen as we were getting ready to leave the house. I thought you might have seen it on TV and I started to call you but decided not to since we were virtually on our way here."

"I haven't had the television on today. I went to the big sale at Grafton's this morning and was busy getting ready for the party most of the afternoon," Jana said in a rush as she sat down in one of the breakfast table chairs. She lowered her head and sat perfectly still. Neither woman spoke for a bit. Finally, Jana raised her head, widened her eyes, and looked at her friend. Shaking her head in a confused manner, she said, "I can't believe what you are saying. I can't believe he is dead. How could that happen?"

"I know," Shirley responded. "The news report said a woman arriving to begin her work shift found him lying in an aisle and called EMS and the police. There weren't any other details reported. The police are asking anyone who saw any suspicious activity in the area to come forward."

Jan knew her reaction was critical. Convincing her friend she didn't know anything about James's murder was the first of many tests she would have to pass. "Oh Shirley, I can't wrap my mind around what you are telling me. I don't know what to think. This is so unreal," she kept shaking her head as she talked.

"I know, Jana. It makes no sense. I'm glad I was the one to tell you though. I was worried that you had heard it on TV and that you were here alone trying to deal with it."

"No, I've been getting ready for the party. I didn't turn the television on," Jana said again, hoping to emphasize she hadn't known.

"I'm glad you didn't find out about it watching television. I've been so worried about you. In spite of everything that happened at the end, he meant a lot to you for many years. It's natural for you to be upset by his death; I wasn't sure how you would feel about it."

"I don't know how I feel," Jana replied, "I suppose shocked and numb would describe it best. And it's funny, but that's the way I've been about James for a long time."

Shirley nodded. She had been Jana's confidante throughout the entire break-up of her marriage. Together they had weathered all the emotions that went with it.

"It's surreal. I can't believe he's gone," Jana purposely spoke quietly projecting an aura of disbelief as once again she shook her head and looked at her friend. "How could he be murdered?"

"I don't know. The news reporter said a full investigation was being launched. Are you all right? Do you want to cancel the party?"

Jana made it a point to wait a moment, appearing to consider what to do before she replied. "No, I don't think so. Everything is ready and the kids are looking forward to it. And besides, as an ex-wife, I'm not sure how I'm supposed to react. Somehow, cancelling my activities doesn't seem appropriate even though I don't want to seem uncaring. Twenty years of sharing your life with someone can't be erased no matter what happens; I'm sure you know I still have feelings for him."

"Oh Jana, I know you do. And you are right. In spite of how your relationship ended and everything you had to endure, there are some good memories. My concern is for you; I just don't want this to send you into a tailspin again."

Jana looked at her friend and a feeling of love and appreciation flooded through her. "You are the best friend in the world, Shirley. You've stood beside me through thick and thin and I love you for it. I'm sure when all this sinks in, I'll have some grief, but right now I'm just trying to process the fact that he is dead." The two friends hugged. "I'll think about this later," she said. "I'm sure it will hit me soon."

The sounding of the doorbell announced the arrival of the first party guests and the two women went to welcome them. Jana and Shirley were leaders of the local children's theatre group and they were celebrating the end of the season which coincided with the local school schedules. Parents, theatre volunteers and the kids themselves were excited about the party. The mood was festive, a fast-paced, joyful occasion. Someone did mention there had been a murder at the lake that afternoon, but no one pursued the subject. Most of the guests had no idea Jana had a connection to the murdered man and the few who knew refrained from speculating about it in front of her.

The embers in the fire pit provided just the right temperature for roasting marshmallows; the kids had a ball making their S'mores and even some of the adults tried their hand at making them. Shirley commented about what a good thing it was that Jan thought about lighting the fire early. Jana remarked again that it was certainly safer than having a blazing fire with all the kids around.

Everyone left before ten o'clock. By all counts, the party had been a huge success. As they were putting away the left-over food,

Jana looked at her friend and sensed she was struggling with how to bring up the subject of her ex-husband's death again.

Deciding it was best for her to initiate the conversation, thoughtfully she offered, "Shirley, I can't put the fact that James is dead out of my mind. Although our marriage has been over for quite a while and he hurt me so much, we did share some good times together. For him to be dead, much less murdered, is just unreal."

"I know. I feel the same way. I don't want to invade your privacy, but will you go to his funeral?"

Once again Jana paused before answering, wanting to make it seem like she was contemplating the question. When she spoke her answer was thoughtful, as if she really didn't know her decision. "I don't think so. It doesn't seem like it would be a good thing. His wife certainly won't want me there and being there would just remind me of his betrayal. I need to give it some thought. I have to absorb all of this. It's a little like being asked for a divorce out of the clear blue; I don't really know how I feel or what I should do."

"I understand. Tell you what; let's go to lunch tomorrow. Don't sit here alone all day. And you know that I will do whatever you want me to do. You are my dearest friend. If you decide to go to the funeral, I'll go with you."

Hearing Shirley's simple statement of loyalty and love brought stinging tears to Jana's eyes. She brushed them away, saying "I'll call you in the morning. Thank you for the millionth time for being my friend," Jana said with emotion.

Shirley hugged her once again, urging her to get some rest and saying she would wait for her call. After exchanging goodbyes, Shirley and her husband left. After watching their car make its way down the street, Jana went upstairs and got ready for bed. Barring all thoughts of the day's activities from her mind and refusing to turn on the television, she crawled into bed, turned off the bedside lamp, and promptly went to sleep.

Chapter 7

Jana awoke a little before seven. Quickly dressing before going to the kitchen, she made coffee and popped a piece of bread in the toaster before retrieving the newspaper from the front porch. She filled her coffee mug and buttered the toasted bread before turning on the television sitting on the kitchen bar and then settled at the breakfast table ready to see what the paper offered. Sure enough, the story about the murder at Taking It Easy was on the front page. Apprehensive about what it would say, she took a deep breath before beginning to read.

According to the article, the police suspected the incident had occurred mid-morning. According to the report, the victim's body had been discovered lying on the floor around noon by an employee reporting for work. A call summoning both an ambulance and the police had been made immediately. A preliminary investigation by the responding officers concluded that nothing in the store had been disturbed. It did not appear that anything had been taken and there were no signs of a struggle. A group of college students who'd rented a boat from the facility had been interviewed but none of them had noticed anything out of the ordinary during the time they were in the store.

The phone rang just as she completed reading. It was Shirley calling to be sure Jana was all right. After a minute or so of conversation, Jana, speaking a little hesitantly, said, "Shirley, you've been through so much with me. You've always been there to support and help. Without your friendship, I don't think I would have made it. You were the one who insisted I go to counseling; without your urging I doubt I would have ever gone and we both know what a difference that made in my life."

Shirley interrupted her friend saying, "Oh Jana, I'm sure you would have realized counseling would help you. I just nudged you in that direction."

Jana laughed and replied, "Maybe I would have but I seriously doubt it. You never lectured or criticized me; you were just there giving me encouragement to start a new life. Your continued care and love made the difference." Jana hoped Shirley was touched by her statements. Then Jana continued, "So, not only are you my best friend, I look to you for guidance. I need your honest opinion about the decision I've made regarding James's death."

Shirley's voice wavered with emotion as she said, "That's what friends are for. You would have done the same for me had the situation been reversed. I promise I will be truthful. What have you decided?"

Jana took a deep breath before speaking. Having Shirley buy into the last part of the plan she had so meticulously constructed was imperative. Quietly, as if she were still contemplating her decision, she began, "I spent most of the night thinking about what I should do. The reality is that my thoughts do not matter; I'm certain any suggestions from me would not be welcomed." Carefully, she continued, "I do not want to act inappropriately but I've decided my initial assessment of whether or not I should attend James's funeral was correct. As I said last evening, his wife certainly won't want me to be there and my presence would just give the gossip mongers fuel for talk. At the same time, I can't, in good conscience, ignore the fact that James died."

Jana paused before continuing, and then almost as if she were explaining to herself rather than to Shirley, Jana said, "You know there was a time when he meant the world to me. Our life together was happy; we shared so many things. The business we built was a special adventure for both of us, a dream come true for him and a challenge for me as I embarked on a retail career. In addition, we traveled to many places and entertained so many friends."

"I well remember those days," Shirley interjected. "You two were the envy of many people. Everyone thought you lived a charmed life."

A soft smile spread across her face as Jana said, "We were married for nineteen years and you, of all people, know how I felt about him. And I do want to honor those good times and the person he was when I fell in love with him. As I thought about our life together, two things stood out in my mind. I kept remembering how much time we spent on the lake. Many times on the weekends, we'd be on the water in time to see the sun either rise or set and discuss every subject imaginable. We both relished the peacefulness those outings brought us. And our other favorite thing to do was work in our rose garden. James loved the roses and although we bought them together, he was the one who did most of the planting and tending them. He was quite an expert gardener. We spent many evenings on the patio having a drink and enjoying the fragrant blossoms. So, I'm thinking an appropriate tribute to him would be for me to gather some roses from our garden and drop them off the bridge that goes over the lake. What do you think?"

Shirley's response was immediate and heartfelt, "Oh Jana, I think that's a fine tribute. It makes perfect sense to me. I know James would be pleased. Do you want me to go with you? I'd be glad to."

Not wanting to rebuff her friend's offer but knowing it was not one she could accept, Jana hesitated and took a deep breath before answering, "Oh Shirley, thank you for offering. I appreciate it very much, but I think I should go alone. It is important for me to do this as a way of saying I've forgiven him. I think it needs to be just between the two of us. Do you understand?" she said, praying her friend would think at long last Jana had resolved her feelings about James and the divorce.

Getting past that hurdle was huge. To reinforce her desire to do something special for James, she said, "It will be the last thing I do for him and I want it to be something we shared."

"You are precious, Jana. It's obvious you've finally put the pain and anger from your divorce behind you. I am so proud of you," Shirley said.

"Maybe I could come by afterward and take you up on your offer that we could go to lunch?" Jana said to let her know she appreciated her concern although she wanted to be alone to do the flowers.

"You do that. I'll be waiting for you," Shirley answered. Jana sighed with relief as she hung up the phone. She drained the last of the coffee from her mug and finished the toast before retrieving the large wicker basket lined with tissue paper sitting on the floor by the back door.

Chapter 8

Stepping outside into the yard, Jana paused taking in the sight before her. Although the roses had just begun blooming the week before, the bushes were already laden with buds and fully-opened flowers. From all indications it was going to be a bountiful season. Methodically going from bush to bush, she focused her full attention on the flowers; she did not allow herself to think about the reason for gathering them.

Painstakingly positioning the blooms in layers over the tissue paper lining, when it was full she made her way to the garage and carefully balanced the basket on the hood of her car before turning toward the bag of potting soil that had been her focus the day before. Once again, she plunged her hand deep inside it, searching for what she'd hidden there. After a moment of digging, she pulled the gun free. It was very dirty; soil clogged the barrel and the carved handle was caked with pieces of the moist potting mixture. Momentary dismay filled her as she gazed at the dirty weapon but then deliberately thrusting aside any concern about its condition, her thoughts immediately turned to the task before her. Very carefully, she slipped the revolver underneath the tissue paper cradling the roses. Just as she had checked the fire pit the night before, she scrutinized the basket from every angle to make sure what needed to be hidden was not visible.

Her next chore was to be sure there was nothing to arouse suspicion should anyone feel it necessary to check the garage. Sweeping the area and re-rolling the top of the potting soil bag left no trace that it had used as a hiding place for a murder weapon. Satisfied with the way things looked, she washed her hands, retrieved her purse from the kitchen and got in the car, her mind focused on the next step of her plan.

The drive to the lake didn't take long; traffic was almost non-existent. It was still too early for sightseers, so no cars were parked in the observation area which was located in the middle of the bridge over the deepest part of the lake. It offered a wonderful place for visitors to stop and view the beautiful surrounding scenery. A sign mounted on a huge boulder detailed the bridge's construction history and pointed out surrounding landmarks. Two benches provided places for sitting and enjoying the peaceful atmosphere.

Jana removed the basket of roses from the car, placing it on the bench closest to the bridge railing. Pretending to enjoy the view, she surveyed the path that bordered the edge of the water to ensure no walkers or hikers were present. Seeing no one, she let her gaze roam over the lake to confirm there were no boats about. The lake was deserted just as it usually was in the early morning.

Two cars passed by on the road as she stood there, but neither slowed down nor seemed to pay her any attention. Once satisfied she was the only person in the area, she gathered several roses from the basket and dropped them over the rail, watching as they drifted through the air and landed on the calm water.

Waiting patiently for them to disappear into the depths of the lake she thought how she would tearfully explain what she was doing if anyone happened to stop before her deed was completed. She smiled as she thought about how it was the perfect cover for getting rid of a very incriminating piece of evidence.

Completing another quick glance around the area and seeing no one, she slipped her hand under the tissue paper and pulled out the gun she'd placed there earlier. Her hand shook slightly as she cradled the precious connection to her father.

"I'm sorry you didn't get cleaned," she whispered. "I know Dad wouldn't be happy with me about that, but I think he'd understand why I didn't follow his instructions. I know that without you I could not have accomplished my task." She felt foolish talking to an inanimate object and even more foolish when she kissed her fingers and brushed them along its handle but somehow it seemed fitting. Knowing it was the last time she'd hold it in her hand, almost reverently she placed the revolver on top of the remaining roses and stood motionless gazing at it for one last time.

Then, with a fluid motion she scooped the remaining flowers along with the gun from the basket, leaned over the rail and dropped the carefully planned tribute to her ex-husband into the lake. The beautiful roses floated through the air along with the revolver. She noticed that the gun didn't look much different from the roses falling toward the water; a casual observer probably would not have noticed it was not a flower, but she still held her breath, watching intently until it splashed on the water and disappeared beneath the lake's surface.

Head bowed as if in prayer, she stood staring at the spot where it had landed, noting that a few of the roses were still peacefully drifting, not yet buried by the water. A glance at her watch revealed the whole episode had lasted less than 10 minutes. Somehow that seemed appropriate; it was more time than James deserved. Briskly, she walked to her car, tossed the basket onto the back floor, got in and drove away without a backwards glance.

Chapter 9

Now that the final act of the plan had been completed, the forty-five-minute drive to Shirley's house gave Jana time to think about the events that had taken place over the past twenty-four hours. In spite of witnessing them happening in her mind many, many, times, it was surreal to her that they had actually occurred. It was true that the ending of her marriage had perpetrated their creation, but it had been the encounter at the wedding which had actually put them into action.

The ending of her marriage had been such a shock, like nothing she'd ever experienced. Her entire life had changed when James told her he wanted a divorce; the world she'd lived in for nineteen years had fallen apart. Utter disbelief, followed by total devastation, had consumed her. There had been no one to turn to; the person who'd guided and supported her through the ups and downs in her world was the very cause of its collapse. "Why did this happen?" and "what am I supposed to do?" were questions with no answers. Helpless and unable to contemplate the next hour, much less the future, life as she'd known it had ended and there had been no desire to find a new one.

Being alone was totally foreign to her; she'd gone from her childhood home to a college environment filled with roommates and then she and James had married. Without ever living independently, she'd never not shared space with someone and she found doing so unpleasant and frightening. The big house that had been so comforting when it was shared with James became a mockery, reminding her at every turn that her life had been a farce.

The business that had consumed so much of her time and energy was now nothing but a reminder that the goals and dreams it promised had no value. Taking It Easy, the sporting goods store and boat rental business, had been the center of their lives, dominating every aspect of it. Begun as James's dream, his fantasy about owning an establishment catering to the outdoors and boating had become a reality with the inheritance she'd gotten when her parents died unexpectedly in a plane crash. Without hesitation, she'd supported buying land and building the sporting goods store he'd dreamed of.

They'd worked so hard, building it together. In addition to her money, she'd poured her heart and soul into its creation. While James concentrated on the boating part of it, the responsibility for the store's operation fell to her. Hours devoted to studying marketing strategies, selecting merchandise, and building displays filled her days and she'd been happy to help make her husband's dream come true.

But suddenly, everything changed. The marriage she'd thought would last a lifetime ended and she'd been caught in an incomprehensible situation, not knowing where to turn or what to do. And while her private world was at a standstill, the one around her continued to function, demanding her attention. There were issues that couldn't wait. James had been relentless in his quest to finalize the divorce forcing her to deal with one issue after the other, to make decisions for which she was totally unprepared. Mired in confusion and grief, she'd been unsure of how to proceed. She'd become a robot, getting through each day mechanically with no real thought about anything.

The turning point had begun one morning as, at wit's end, wandering aimlessly from room to room, she'd decided to go to Taking It Easy, thinking it might bring some sense of normalcy to her world. She remembered arriving there and trying to find some motivation, something to spark her into an activity, but that after a brief conversation with the clerk, it had become plain the store didn't offer any solutions to her dilemma. She'd actually been preparing to leave when James walked through the door. Without a greeting, he'd addressed her almost formally, asking "Jana, can we sit down and talk? We need to settle some things."

Remembering not having a clue what he wanted to discuss and also recalling the weariness that enveloped her at the prospect of yet another confrontation with him, she'd muttered, "All right."

They'd sat on the tall stools behind the check-out counter, a place where they often ended their business day, having a drink and discussing activities and for a moment, the familiarity of being there had given her hope he'd changed his mind about the divorce. But then he'd pulled a sheet of paper from his pocket and laid it on the counter. His condescending tone still echoed in her mind as did his pitying look as he'd pretended what he was doing was best for her.

"You need to sign this agreement," he'd said decisively. "We both know running this business is too much for you. It's time for you to pursue other interests."

Recalling how, that after hearing his declaration she'd not responded, and also remembering that evidently her silence had angered him, prompting his next words, "No woman can be in charge of a sporting goods venture."

Time had not erased the astonishment his statement evoked. It jarred her from the depths of despair and aimlessness she'd been mired in for weeks. With a simple sentence, he'd dismissed everything she'd done to make their business a success, giving her no credit for the thriving enterprise it was. She'd sat there, stunned by his biased observation.

"I'm sure you will find something else to do," he'd added, as he'd pushed the document closer to her and laid a pen on the counter. In a flash, the realization James had every intention of stripping Taking It Easy from her, claiming it as solely his had become crystal clear.

Even after all the elapsed time, she remembered how in that instant, his words struck the right chord to put his betrayal, the dissolution of their marriage, the business, and her need to move forward in proper perspective. She'd stood up, cleared her throat and announced in a clear, firm voice, "I have nothing to say to you James nor am I signing anything. From now on, you need to deal with my attorney." Thinking how ironic it was that James' own words were the catalyst for her to face reality and take control. Looking at herself in the car's rearview mirror, she said aloud, "That was the beginning of getting my life back, and today was the ending of my dealings with James Browning."

Chapter 10

As she continued driving, Jana silently acknowledged rebuilding her life had not been easy. Letting her thoughts return to those first months, when she'd had to face the reality of being single, made her shudder. Used to having a husband to share her life, especially making important decisions, facing life-changing issues alone and not having him to discuss things with or guide her through the process left her unsure of every choice she'd made. To make things even harder, the choices she had to make involved confrontations with the very man who had been her confidante, the one she'd trusted, the very one she'd loved with all her heart.

Had it not been for best friend Shirley who, fulfilling the roles of confider, encourager, task assistant, and sounding board for all her issues and concerns, had played a major role in her return to reality, she probably would not have been able to move forward. Thinking about all the ways Shirley had helped her, including being there for her today, brought tears to her eyes. Shirley had always been willing to listen, offering suggestions and solutions to issues which had overwhelmed her. It had been Shirley who insisted an attorney needed to be involved in the divorce settlement negating James's claim that one was not needed.

Jana remembered one of the first decisions Shirley helped with was where she should live. Shortly before the wedding, her parents had given the house she and James lived in to her. When her father handed her the deed, he'd made it very clear she was the sole owner so there was no controversy over it during the divorce. But she remembered confiding to Shirley that staying there was not possible because it brought unbearable memories. She'd shared that the biggest issue was the master bedroom, explaining she didn't want to go into it, much less sleep in the bed she'd shared with James.

Shirley's solution, a total make-over included replacing the wall in the bedroom with a huge picture window looking out into the yard, re-painting and re-carpeting and replacing every piece of the furniture. When it was finished it bore no resemblance to what she'd shared with James. Throughout the house changes were made: new counters and cabinets in the bathroom, along with new flooring and lighting transformed it completely. New living room furniture, except for her baby grand piano and a desk that had belonged to her mother, added to the transformation. The front yard make-over included removing shrubs, planting flowers, adding a rock wall, and re-doing the driveway, creating a different look from what it had been. In the end, there was nothing to bring back memories. It was beautiful and comforting; it was also totally hers.

As she mentally reviewed all the issues Shirley had helped her with, the realization that the most important assistance she had provided was something neither of them had realized at the time. Playing the long-ago conversation that had prompted its instigation over in her mind, there was no doubt that at the time she thought it was her gift to Shirley, never dreaming the importance it would have for her.

It had begun one morning after a particularly difficult night; she recalled the telephone conversation clearly. She'd shared with Shirley how scared and nervous she was being alone at night and how she'd said, "Noises I never before noticed keep me awake. I'm so scared; I don't feel safe at all. I don't know how to get over it."

Shirley had made some soothing comment about how it would get better as time went on and she'd thought the subject was closed. However, that afternoon Shirley appeared and made an announcement. "I've made an appointment for us this afternoon."

Curious, thinking it was for a pedicure or massage, she'd asked, "Where are we going?"

Recalling Shirley's response, she acknowledged that at the time she'd not had a clue the impact it would have on her. "We're going to the gun shop where both of us will buy pistols and enroll in their class in Women's Self-defense." Enthusiastically, she'd confided, "I've always wanted to take one of those courses. This is a perfect opportunity for me to do it, and it will help you too."

Jana remembered how her first reaction had been to tell Shirley she already knew self-defense; that her dad had insisted she take lessons at a firing range and that he'd also left her a revolver, but as she'd started to explain, Shirley, assuming a refusal was coming, interrupted her saying, "Please don't say you won't take the class or buy a gun; just do it for me. I don't want to take the course alone."

She'd been touched by that simple plea from her dear friend who'd done so much for her. Thinking it was a small way for her to repay Shirley for all her help, she'd squelched the words she'd planned to say and agreed to the proposal, not offering the information she was proficient with guns or that she owned a revolver. Shirley had been so delighted. They'd had so much fun taking the self-defense course together, both buying Ruger 380 automatics. Throughout the class, she'd been careful to portray herself as an inexperienced student.

Every step of the way, Shirley had been such a blessing, never criticizing or judgmental in any way, even when she'd been angry or inappropriate. When their friends were shocked by Jana's vehement statement, "I'd rather see him dead than married to that sales rep," and questioned Shirley about it, her quiet explanation that it was just an off-hand comment meant to describe the enormity of the hurt James's actions had caused thwarted any further speculation. As she drove, Jana mused how it was mind boggling that the random comment so fiercely defended by her best friend had actually morphed into the action that had just taken place.

During the many sleepless nights in the midst of all the drama associated with the divorce proceedings, somehow, between midnight and dawn, countless scenarios of how James's demise might be accomplished had run through her mind. Exploring those possibilities had been a kind of therapy for her. At the time, she'd never actually considered committing murder; but considering how his death might happen had been a way to combat the heart wrenching pain that seared her every day. It had also supplied a measure of satisfaction that justice could be served.

As time passed, the support of good friends, especially Shirley, and the intense counseling she'd recommended had led her away from dwelling on her pain and loss, moving her focus away from the divorce toward new goals and activities.

Well aware that she'd never understand why her marriage ended, eventually she'd dealt with the fact that it had. The visions of eliminating James had dimmed as she moved ahead to new adventures although the detailed, thought-out plans of how it might be accomplished were firmly embedded in her brain alongside the hurt he'd caused her.

Chapter 11

Maneuvering the car through the light traffic, Jana's thoughts continued to review the journey she'd traveled, ending with the morning's culminating act. It was really ironic that such a joyous occasion, the wedding of a long-time friend's daughter, had been the impetus for it.

Originally, she and Shirley planned to attend the festivities together, but her friend had to cancel at the last minute. Going alone had not been at all appealing and she'd considered skipping it but having been friends with the bride's mother for many years and watching the bride grow up, she'd felt it was important to be there for her.

The ceremony had been beautiful and, for the most part, enjoyable. It stirred up memories of her wedding when the future looked so bright and the promise "till death do you part" had been spoken without any doubt that it would be kept. Briefly, the grief she'd so carefully overcome threatened to resurface but she'd firmly put all thoughts of the past out of her mind as, along with the other guests, she'd begun making her way to the reception being held in the church's parlor. She was determined to concentrate on the bride's and groom's joy, putting aside thoughts of her by gone days.

Going through the reception line, the bride's smile and appreciative words erased all misgivings she'd had about attending the wedding. They'd chatted briefly, reliving memories and parted with a hug. Making her way through the crowd to the buffet table, she'd been glad to be part of the celebration. That's when she'd seen James and his wife across the room. Startled by their presence, James was not particularly close to the family and his new wife certainly didn't know them, it never occurred to her that they might be there.

For a moment she hadn't known what to do. Hoping to escape without being spotted, she'd turned to leave but was detained by a friend she hadn't seen in a while. There was no polite way to avoid visiting with him. And as luck would have it, when their conversation ended and she'd started to walk toward the exit, James and his wife were just a few feet from her. His wife was busy talking to someone and hadn't seen her, but James had.

He didn't acknowledge her. He didn't speak, nor did he nod or smile, but there was no doubt he'd seen her. His eyes had locked with hers for a long moment, his expression almost taunting. It crossed her mind that she should speak to him, but before any words were formed, he'd turned away, draping his arm around his wife's shoulders, pulling her close to him and planting a kiss on her cheek.

It had been a deliberate slap in Jana's face. Seeing him bestow the same affection he'd once shown to her to someone else was overwhelming and the buried hatred she'd experienced during the divorce had once again consumed her. It was at that moment she'd realized that she would never be free from his mockery. Shaken to her very core, the anger she'd so carefully learned to control surged through her with a vengeance more violent than it had ever been. Although every part of her wanted to confront his arrogance, she'd managed to control her impulse and made her way out of the building. Sitting in her car shaking from head to toe, the picture of him caressing his newfound love played over and over in her mind. Finally, she was able to calm herself enough to drive.

Once home, she'd tried hard to convince herself he didn't matter, that her new life was fulfilling. But, the realization that being free from the pain and agony caused by his betrayal would never be accomplished as long as the possibility she'd have to deal with his presence remained.

Later that evening, after re-playing his actions in her head, she made her decision. Pulling a legal pad from the kitchen drawer, she devised a timeline for the plan that had been embedded in her brain during the many sleepless nights following his betrayal. Strangely enough, there had been no debate in her mind as to whether she should proceed. She'd known that there was no way she wanted to live her life in constant dread of seeing him somewhere.

And knowing for the plan to be successful, certain conditions were necessary didn't matter. Waiting until the time was right gave her opportunity to gather everything that was needed and to replay its every detail over and over. On a weekend trip to the coast, she'd started by accumulating the dark wig and make-up, along with the leggings and long t-shirt that would be her outfit for the trip to Taking It Easy. Buying them with cash, there was no way to trace their purchase to her. The large tote bag came from a display in a Walgreen's store and the canvas shoes she'd also gotten there were a size larger than the ones she wore. They could be carefully made to fit her feet by stuffing the toes with crumpled tissue paper.

Over and over, she painstakingly rehearsed every action required to completely change her appearance. She practiced putting the wig on, re-shaping her eyebrows with the black pencil, and making her lips look fuller with the dark lipstick until she could alter her looks in a matter of minutes.

Waiting for the right time had been an exercise in patience but finally the circumstances aligned. The theatre group, she and her friend Shirley directed, dismissed for the summer and they scheduled a party at her house for all its students. The local newspaper contained ads for boat rentals from Taking It Easy, the rose garden was coming alive with beautiful blooms and Grafton's had announced their big end-of-season sale. And she'd been ready; there had been no hesitation on her part. Her patience had been rewarded. She executed the entire plan without one hitch.

However, the reality of it was overwhelming. Stopping the car in the driveway at Shirley's house, Jana was surprised to find her hands were shaking so hard she could hardly pull the key from the ignition. Pulling a wet wipe from the carton on the seat beside her, she deftly wiped her hands to erase any trace of dirt from the revolver that might remain on them. Inhaling deeply, she forced herself to concentrate on what to say to her friend before she opened the car door and stepped onto the driveway. Clumsily, she made her way to the front door and rang the bell. Shirley opened it immediately, and immersed Jana in a huge hug.

"How are you?" Shirley asked, as she held Jana tightly.

Jana tried to respond but all the pent-up emotions she'd held in check for so long prevented an answer. Trembling, she held onto her friend without speaking. Gently, Shirley led her to the couch. As Jana sank down into its soft cushions, she buried her head in her hands. Sobs shook her body as tears flowed down her cheeks. Her tears were not ones of sorrow, but of relief that her mission was finally completed.

PART TWO

Chapter 12

Detective Mike Stone eased his six-foot frame into the swivel chair behind the desk, took a sip of coffee from the mug he'd filled in the break room and let his thoughts ponder the new case he and his partner, Jack Beatty, had been assigned to handle. The call summoning them to the popular Lake City Park shopping complex the day before had come after lunch. One of the business owners, James Browning, had been fatally shot in his store.

Thinking about their initial visit to the scene, he remembered that by the time he and Jack arrived, police had already secured the site and conducted a preliminary investigation. The information Sergeant Winters, the officer in charge, shared with them was sketchy at best. He said that Mr. Browning had been discovered lying on the floor by an employee reporting to work, who'd immediately called both EMS and the police. In response to their question regarding the employee's statement, they'd been directed to the end of one of the aisles where a woman was sitting. Mike, always observant, studied her carefully as they made their way across the store. His first impression was that she was older than he'd anticipated the person being. He guessed she was about 60, which was a little surprising. For some reason, he'd assumed a younger person would be employed in a sporting goods store. She'd nodded, identifying herself as Cora Landing when they'd introduced themselves and he explained their role in investigating the incident. Clearly upset, Ms. Landing had red eyes, trembling hands, and her cheeks bore the trace of tears.

Mike punched the "play" button on his cell phone and listened as the recorded conversation began. Ms. Landing's voice was shaky as she recounted finding James Browning. "I got here a few minutes before one o'clock which is when my shift begins. The "open" sign in the window was lit and I came in and, as usual, put my purse in the small safe on the counter under the cash register. I didn't see Mr. Browning, so I called out to let him know I'd arrived. Getting no reply, I assumed he was in the back room gathering extra merchandise to be added to the shelves. I began making my way back there and that's when I saw him on the floor."

"What was his condition?" Mike's voice was clear on the recording.

"He was just lying there. His eyes were open, and he wasn't moving or making any sound," the recording continued. "There was blood all around him and he didn't respond to me when I leaned over him and said his name."

"What did you do? Did you touch him or move anything close to him"?

"No, I didn't touch him and there was nothing around him; he was just on the floor. From what I saw, he was beyond any help I could give him. I ran to the telephone and called 911."

Mike's voice asked, "Did you see anyone on the premises?" the recording continued.

Ms. Landing's voice was firm as she replied, "There was no one in the store but that isn't unusual in the middle of the day. Most of our customers come in the morning or late in the afternoon when the boat rentals are done. It's usually slow in between."

Her response to his questions about James Browning included what a good-hearted, down-to-earth person he was. Mike recalled that it wasn't until he'd ask for the tape from the surveillance camera, that she'd said anything remotely negative about her boss.

Remembering how the tone of her voice had become a little accusatory as she'd shaken her head and answered, "The camera has been broken for months. I told Mr. Browning about it and even reminded him several times, but he didn't seem at all concerned that it wasn't working," Mike detected a slight note of disdain. And then she'd added a comment, "I can tell you for sure that if Mrs. Browning had still been here, she would have reacted immediately and had it fixed. But that's the difference between the two of them. She's the one who tended things; he left everything to her. It's been a different place since she isn't here."

Her strongly-voiced opinion made Mike wonder what had happened to cause Mrs. Browning's absence. But before he could pursue the subject, almost as if she'd regretted voicing any criticism, Ms. Landing had bowed her head and began crying quietly, so he'd not questioned her further. Giving her his card, he told her to contact either him or Jack if she thought of anything further that might shed light on the incident.

Thoughtfully he reviewed the brief notes in front of him. They didn't offer much information at all; the first speculation was that the murder was a robbery gone awry, but there were problems with that theory because, as far as anyone could tell, nothing had been taken from the store. It had not been ransacked; all the merchandise was neatly displayed. In addition, there was money, three hundred dollars plus some change in the cash register, along with a credit card transaction showing a boat rental. Those two facts, the lack of disorder and the presence of money, belied the robbery motive.

And the murder scene itself was puzzling. The victim had been shot twice at close range and there were no signs of any kind of struggle. That suggested two possibilities: either he knew the shooter, or he had been caught off guard and completely surprised before he had a chance to defend himself. No evidence of any kind had been found; there were no bloody footprints around the scene, and no trace of anyone having been there. It was disappointing that there was no surveillance tape to capture what happened.

His thoughts turned to the trip he and Jack made accompanying the police to tell the man's widow the bad news. Although those visits were never pleasant, this one had been exceptionally difficult. Mrs. Browning had been apprehensive when she opened the door and saw him and Jack and two uniformed officers standing there. When Jack told her that there had been an incident at the store, she'd become apprehensive. "Where's James?" she'd asked nervously.

Jack suggested they go inside and reluctantly she agreed. When she heard the words, 'I'm sorry to tell you Mr. Browning was shot,' she'd immediately asked, "Which hospital was he taken to?" When Mike responded quietly that he was sorry, but his wounds had been fatal, she began screaming, becoming completely hysterical. There was no calming her down. No matter what they did, she was uncontrollable.

Finally, a neighbor who'd noticed the police cars in front of the house came to see what was happening. She'd finally gotten Mrs. Browning to quit screaming, but her sobbing had continued. There had been no opportunity for further discussion.

A brief conversation with the neighbor revealed that the couple had not been married very long; the neighbor thought around a year or so. She'd offered that Mrs. Browning was significantly younger than her husband and that there were no children. She didn't think they had near-by relatives, but she wasn't sure. Mrs. Browning had finally calmed down enough to give them a name and telephone number to contact a friend and the neighbor assured them she'd stay until the person arrived.

As he re-examined everything, Mike remembered that as he and Jack had driven away, he'd noted that the Browning's house was very expensive. Ultra-modern, it was very large with an immaculate front lawn that was beautifully landscaped. He also recalled seeing a magnificent patio and swimming pool through the expansive picture window across the living room wall when they were inside. And the part they'd been in was exquisitely decorated. Everything about it suggested the couple was well heeled financially; it spoke of wealth. He also recalled Ms. Landing's description of Mrs. Browning, saying she was the one who took care of everything. In his opinion, it didn't fit at all with the person he'd spent the last two hours with.

His thoughts turned to the business where the murder occurred. Taking It Easy was the most unique enterprise in the shopping complex. Located at the end of the lake, it featured a large dock where boats and paddle boards were housed with the store next to it offering a vast array of sporting supplies and equipment. The last establishment on the street, it was somewhat isolated but still part of the main activity.

There certainly wasn't much to go on. But in his twenty-seven years as a detective, there had been many cases without any initial leads, and he was confident something would materialize that would point to the culprit. Resigned to the fact that they would start with the basics and go step by step, he decided his first step was to talk to the person who'd signed the credit card voucher and arrange a meeting with him. He reached for the telephone, ready to begin the process.

Chapter 13

The next morning as he and Jack walked into the conference room and greeted the young man standing beside the long table, he was reminded that this was probably the last person James Browning had spent time with before he was killed. Tall, tanned, and obviously very nervous, Mike concentrated on putting him at ease.

"Jeff Summers?" he asked pleasantly, "I'm Mike Stone and this is my partner, Jack Beatty. Thank you for coming in."

"It's no problem," the young man replied. "I was shocked to hear of Mr. Browning's death. My friends and I enjoyed meeting him. He seemed like a really neat guy."

Methodically, Mike began asking questions. Jeff answered readily, recounting how he and his friends had gone to Taking It Easy to see about renting a boat for the coming weekend. He said they met James Browning at the boat dock and discussed the different rentals available. After deciding on the boat they wanted to rent, James had suggested they go ahead and take the rental agreement to complete, saying it would save them time when they came to get it. They'd gone into the store, signed the papers and paid the rental fee by credit card, which they were told would not be processed until after the boat had actually been used.

When questioned whether anyone else had been nearby, Jeff offered that a woman entered the business at the same time as he and his friends, adding he'd held the door open for her. When probed about her, Jeff said she had paused just inside the front door and looked around the store, finally centering her attention on the display of sunscreen by the entrance. His description of her was vague. He said she had dark short hair and was wearing pants and a t-shirt. "Did she act suspicious in any way?" Mike asked. "Was she still in the store when you went to get the boat?"

Jeff's expression was thoughtful as he said, "No, I got the impression it wasn't the type of store she thought it was. She kept gazing all around as if to see what was there, but she didn't walk down any of the aisles or anything. I'm fairly certain she didn't stay there very long; she probably left when she saw what the store had to offer. I didn't actually see her leave, but I didn't see her anywhere when we left."

"Did Mr. Browning say anything to her? Was there interaction between the two of them?"

"No, I'm certain of that," Jeff said. "He could have thought she was with us since she came in when we did, but I don't know that for sure. His whole attention was on answering questions about the boat and telling us about different routes to use exploring the lake."

According to Jeff, after all the necessary paperwork had been completed for the upcoming weekend, James had encouraged them to take the boat out for a bit to get used to how it handled. Jeff estimated they were on the lake for no more than 45 minutes. "We didn't see Mr. Browning when we brought the boat back, but he'd told us if he wasn't there to dock it in the same slip we'd gotten it from, and drop the keys in the lock box. And that's what we did."

Mike thanked Jeff for his time and gave him his business card before saying goodbye. Although it really didn't offer any pertinent information, Mike made a detailed report of their meeting.

As the investigation continued, he conducted interviews with people in the businesses closet to Taking It Easy. According to everyone they spoke with, there hadn't been any unusual or suspicious activity in the area. One of the men questioned said there had been a loud noise that might have been a gunshot but explained that at the time he heard it he'd assumed it was one of the boats backfiring out on the lake. No useful information came from the other shop owners. Without exception, everyone they talked to reported the same things about James Browning. Over and over, they heard he was a good neighbor.

"He was easy-going, very laid back, always willing to lend a hand," was one man's description of the murdered man and that pretty well summed up how everyone felt. More than one person mentioned how both James and his wife had worked tirelessly in the Taking It Easy store. Somehow Mike had a problem thinking the woman he'd met the day James died was the type of person who would work tirelessly anywhere, especially in a sporting goods establishment, but it didn't seem important.

Chapter 14

The two detectives diligently pursued the task of solving James Browning's murder. Methodically, they contacted friends and associates. Although Mrs. Browning furnished most of the names, Ms. Landing supplied a list of those connected with the business. Conversations with those didn't reveal anything suspicious or unusual. It wasn't until one of the vendors, who commented that things had really changed with the operation of the store since his former wife didn't work there any longer, that Mike realized there was more than one Mrs. Browning. Further probing confirmed James had divorced and remarried, and that the person he and his partner, Jack, had met was the new wife. That information was noted in the file, although it did not appear to have any bearing on the case.

Since, according to Mrs. Browning, Ray Schuller was James's best friend and knew him better than anyone else, they decided to meet with him first. In response to Mike's call, Ray immediately agreed to come to the office that afternoon.

When he arrived, introductions were made, and the three men proceeded to the conference room. Noting that Ray was well dressed and immaculately groomed, Mike surmised that he was an executive of some sort. Once they were seated, Mike explained, "Quite frankly, we are at a loss. The crime scene is pristine, there is no evidence of anything being taken from the store and no one noticed anything out of the ordinary. We're talking with all of Mr. Browning's friends in the hopes someone might furnish a clue as to why it happened. So, if you could just talk about him and the relationship you shared, especially anything unusual you noticed lately, we'd appreciate it."

Without hesitation Ray began, "James was a laid back, easy-going person. We've been friends since college. I was best man in his wedding, and he was also mine."

"Do you work together?" Mike asked.

"No, after college James became involved in the boating business and I pursued a career in financial planning. James would never have tolerated spending all his time in an office and I could never abide being outside all day," Ray offered with a smile.

Mike nodded, thinking he'd been right about Ray. "Do you have any ideas about why someone would kill him?" Mike asked, carefully observing the man before him. "Did he mention any conflict to you?"

"No, it makes no sense to me," Ray replied as he shook his head. "James was the most ordinary person in the world. He fit the description of "average" more than anyone I can think of."

"Did you notice anything at all that was different about him in the past few months?" Mike asked.

"No, but I haven't seen him very often lately," he admitted, adding, "we sort of drifted apart the last couple of years."

Noting a slight change in his demeanor, Mike asked, "Did something happen to cause an estrangement?"

"Not anything between the two of us," Ray said, "but a couple of years ago James divorced his first wife and remarried a much younger woman. It was something none of our social group remotely expected, nor saw coming. We were all stunned when it happened."

"So, there weren't any signs that his marriage was in trouble?" Mike asked congenially.

Firmly Ray answered, "No, there was nothing to arouse any suspicion about the marriage."

"How did you find out about the split?" Mike asked. "Was the divorce congenial? Did he and his wife just decide to end their marriage?"

For a moment, Ray didn't respond. As Mike watched him closely, it was obvious he was choosing his words very carefully. In a quiet voice, he said, "It was complicated. His wife was not expecting the marriage to end any more than the rest of us. In addition to changing her life, it had a profound effect on all of us. Everything we'd shared through the years, including holiday celebrations, summer trips and even everyday backyard barbeques, were completely different. It was quite a blow to discover someone you thought you knew so well was really someone you didn't know at all."

Chapter 15

Mike observed the man sitting across from him carefully. It crossed his mind that Ray Schuller was a good man, someone who would be a good friend. He felt there was more to the story about James Browning's divorce than he was telling. Cautiously he asked, "So how did you feel when you learned the marriage was ending? Were you surprised?"

"Shocked would be a better description. My wife and I were with them a lot; we spent time on the lake together, went to the theatre, had dinner fairly often, took trips together and took turns being in each other's homes. We were very close. But I guess not as close as we thought because neither of us saw any indication that the marriage was troubled."

Changing the subject, Mike asked, "Did you know his wife before they married?"

Ray smiled as he answered, "Yes, I've also known Jana since college. James picked a winner in every sense of the word when he chose her for his wife. She's a great person. And she fell for James hook, line and sinker."

"Did James offer any explanation as to why the marriage didn't last?" Mike asked.

"Not really. It was as if he knew no one would believe anything negative about Jana and, he was too busy trying to impress all of us with his new bride," Ray spoke with a hint of criticism.

"Did he offer any information about the divorce proceedings?" Mike asked.

"No. Early on, he did complain to me about Jana's demands in the divorce agreement, but I made it very clear I didn't want to become part of that discussion. And I never did."

Mike sensed that Ray was uncomfortable talking about the divorce and decided to change focus.

"What about his new wife?" Mike asked. "What is she like?"

Ray shifted in his chair, looked down for a minute and then spoke, saying, "She's quite a bit younger than James and very different from Jana. She's flashy, loud, and very opinionated. She likes being the center of attention. To be perfectly honest, since his marriage to her, I haven't seen him very much." He looked at Mike before continuing, "It was always James and Jana, and getting used to it being James and someone else wasn't something I cared to do. None of us in the group of friends knew how to react to the divorce, especially the wives. The few times my wife and I were with them socially were awkward at best. So, we drifted apart. The sad part of the situation is that, in addition to becoming somewhat alienated from James, we lost Jana too."

"Do you not see her anymore?" Mike asked.

"We've seen her some. At first, she was completely out of touch with all of us. The whole thing was extremely hard for her; it wasn't easy being around the people the two of them spent time with, so she avoided those situations. I did contact her best friend, Shirley, to see if there was any way I could help her, but at the time Shirley said there was nothing anyone could do. She did contact me sometime later to let tell me Jana was seeing a counselor and that she was better."

They talked for a few more minutes before ending the interview. Ray promised to contact them should he think of anything that might be pertinent and furnished a list of other friends they might want to interview.

The task of interviewing James's friends continued, but nothing new was discovered. Everyone had the same thing to say: James was a great guy, a good friend, honest, and always willing to help. His life had been ordinary, according to his closest acquaintances, except for the ending of his first marriage. Everyone indicated what a surprise the divorce had been; the couple appeared to be happy. No one had an inkling that the marriage was in trouble.

More than one said how devoted his first wife had been, how she'd worked tirelessly building their business and how supportive she was of anything James wanted. Their admiration for her was unanimous.

None of them had suspected he was involved with another woman. Without fail, they all expressed their shock over the divorce and his quick remarriage. In spite of his actions, he maintained his friendships with them, even though the former closeness and camaraderie between the couples cooled, because his first wife was no longer part of the group.

Idly, Mike's thoughts turned to the ex-wife. They always added interest to a case. He wondered exactly how nasty the divorce had been; from Ray's comments it was his bet that it had been pretty heated. In addition, he was very curious about the financial settlement. Putting his coffee cup down and picking up the pad from his desk, he made a note to investigate the former Mrs. Browning.

Chapter 16

Ironically, it was the interview with the last person, Oscar Nelson, who was the owner of the coffee shop James and his friends often frequented, named on the list Mrs. Browning gave to him that deepened Mike's interest in the ex-wife. He and Jack had gone to the establishment unannounced. It was mid-morning and other than a few customers sitting at the long counter, the place was deserted. After introducing themselves to Oscar, they were ushered to a table near the rear of the building. Once again Mike went through the explanation about investigating James's murder and contacting people who knew him.

"Tell us about James. What kind of guy was he?" Mike asked.

"He was a regular guy," Oscar answered offering, "the kind who would do anything for you, just an all-around good person. He was well liked; always pleasant and enjoyed being with his friends."

Do you know of any problems he was experiencing?" Jack asked.

"No, as far as I know his business was going great; James loved being with the boats. He was fair in his dealings with people and had many return customers."

"Did you know of any enemies, anyone who was angry with him or anything like that?" Mike queried.

"No, I'm not aware of anyone but my contact with him was mostly here in the coffee shop," Oscar said.

"Can you think of anyone who had an issue with him; any kind of beef about anything?" Mike asked.

"No, I wasn't aware of anything like that," he said. For a moment Oscar was silent, and then, laughing and shaking his head, he said jokingly, "Now if the murder had occurred when he and his first wife were going through their divorce, my answer might have been different. She would have been a good suspect."

"Oh?" Mike said. "Why do you say that?"

Oscar responded, "James told me she was very angry, and had made statements that she'd 'rather see him dead than married to that sales rep.'" He concluded by adding, "James mentioned she'd bought a gun and taken lessons to learn to shoot it. I told him he needed to be careful, but he laughed and said she was much too proper and classy to commit murder." Oscar sat quietly for a minute before adding, "I told him she might be too classy to kill him herself, but she just might hire somebody to do the job for her."

"Do you think his ex-wife had anything to do with his death?" Mike asked, his tone serious.

"Nah, I was just joking with him; he wasn't at all concerned about her. From what I know about her, she is too classy to do anything like that."

Although Oscar insisted his comment was a joke, Mike wasn't amused. There just might be more to it. As he and his partner left the shop, Mike wondered exactly what kind of person James Browning's ex-wife really was. It seemed to be an established fact that a long legal battle had ensued as the couple worked to divide their assets. Evidentially his ex-wife had driven a hard bargain and was relentless in what she wanted. He also remembered being told that it had taken a good while for the divorce agreement to be reached.

And from conversations with various people, Mike had also learned that she was instrumental in their business, that it was her ideas, her research, and her money that got it started. And more than one person had pointed out that the success of the sporting goods store was due to her. She was the one who selected the merchandise, did the displays, and spent hours making sure all aspects of the operation were in order. Mike remembered the comment Ms. Landing had made about the surveillance camera being out of order, and how James Browning had ignored the problem, instead of tending to it as his wife would have done. One friend had summed up his evaluation of the former Mrs. Browning by saying, "She's a tough woman, super intelligent and very capable. For her to demand a generous settlement was not surprising."

Reviewing the interview notes, Mike was struck by how everyone had said the same thing. It made him think that James's friends had gotten together and outlined what they would say about him; their descriptions were practically identical. Mike wondered if there was something they all wanted to keep hidden about him. It made no sense that not one of them had suspected James Browning's marriage was in trouble or that he was seeing another woman. It also made no sense that every one of them was adamant that James had no issues with anyone. Surely, he would have told at least one friend about a problem. Mike wondered if they were all involved in some illegal activity and were protecting one another. There was no evidence of that, but for everyone to respond to his questions in the very same manner was certainly unusual and a little suspect. It was something certainly worth exploring.

Sighing, he shifted his thoughts to Jana Browning. He admitted being intrigued about her. From everything he'd heard, she was almost a saint. Obviously, her husband hadn't shared the same opinion of her. It was interesting that the marriage everyone thought was so perfect hadn't lasted. She was already on their interview list, but having heard Oscar's comments, Mike's interest in her piqued. He decided a surprise visit would be the thing to do and sent an email to Jack informing him of the upcoming visit. Once again, he thought about how, sometimes, unexpected interviews brought impromptu responses which revealed useful information.

Chapter 17

Although Jana was not certain it would happen, she was fairly confident the authorities handling James's death would want to talk to her. To be prepared, she conducted mock interviews with herself before the bathroom mirror, posing every question she could think of that might be asked, so there would be no surprises to catch her off-guard. In addition, she carefully followed her usual schedule, making sure her routine was unchanged, to avoid any speculation that something about her was amiss since James's death. She stayed close to home, working in the yard, cleaning the fire pit, and just sitting by the pool; biding her time, waiting to be contacted.

So, when the doorbell rang unexpectedly in the middle of the morning, and she saw two men through the door's stained glass, there was no doubt in her mind who they were. Before going to answer it, she deliberately straightened her shoulders and cast a quick glance around the immaculate living room to be sure everything was in order. Greeting them cordially as she opened the door, they immediately showed their badges and introduced themselves. With a quizzical look on her face, in a puzzled tone, she asked how she could help them.

"We are investigating the murder of James Browning," Mike's partner explained. "We'd like to come in and talk to you."

"Of course, come in," she said, opening the door wider for them to enter. She led them to the living room and indicated they should sit on the sofa, before asking, "Can I get you something to drink?"

"No, thank you," Jack answered, taking the lead. "We won't take much of your time."

Jana nodded and sat down in one of the chairs across from the sofa, waiting for them to begin.

"You are aware that Mr. Browning was shot in his store," Mike Stone said matter-of-factly, watching her closely to see her reaction.

"Yes, I'm aware of that," she said without a trace of any emotion, "Do you know what happened?"

"Well, at this point, we really don't know anything except that he was shot," Mike answered, carefully observing her. "Can you tell me when you learned of his death?"

"It was in the evening on the day he died. My friend, Shirley Lewis, told me," she said. "We were hosting a party here that night, and when she arrived around seven o'clock, just before the party, she told me."

"I see," the detective commented.

"I suppose it was a robbery," she stated, looking at Mike.

"We don't think so; nothing was taken, as far as anyone can tell," he answered, before asking, "When was the last time you saw or spoke to him, Mrs. Browning?"

Mike noticed an immediate change in Jana's friendly demeanor. Raising her head somewhat defiantly, she addressed him, "Detective, please know that my name is no longer Browning; I changed it back to Arnold, my maiden name, when the divorce was final." Mike noted her firmness as she offered that piece of information.

"I'm sorry," he offered. "Our records didn't reflect that."

"Please correct them. Browning no longer has any connection with me," Jana said and then, dismissing the subject, she continued, answering his question. "Let's see, you asked about when I saw, or spoke to James last. That would have been several months ago at the wedding of the daughter of one of our friends. He and his wife were there. I saw them from a distance. We did not speak. Pardon me, but may I ask why I am being questioned?"

"We are contacting everyone who knew Mr. Browning," Mike offered.

"I see," Jana said.

"Hopefully, someone will have information that will help us find out who killed him," he replied as he surveyed the woman sitting opposite him. Once again, well aware that spontaneous responses sometimes supplied clues or motives that were otherwise undetected, his observation skills were in full swing as he carefully watched her reaction. He noted that she slowly smoothed her skirt before speaking.

"I don't think I can help you, Detective. Except for seeing him at the wedding, which was entirely accidental, I've had no contact with James since our divorce settlement was signed. I was surprised that he was at the wedding. And to be perfectly candid with you, I would not have attended had I known he was going to be there."

That bit of added information was both unexpected and surprising. "So, your divorce was not amicable?" he asked.

Raising her chin, she stared at him for a moment without blinking, not saying anything. He noted that she was a very attractive woman, with a flawless complexion and beautiful brown eyes. Remembering Ray Shuller's words describing the current Mrs. Browning, it crossed his mind that Jana was not at all like James Browning's widow. From her hesitancy, he knew she was considering how to answer his inquiry. When she did speak, her voice was controlled and firm, without a hint of animosity.

"Detective Stone, I am going to speak frankly to you. If you are interviewing everyone who knew James, you already know, or will soon learn, all about what happened anyway. When the news surfaced that James was divorcing me, it was the topic of all our friend's conversations. It was quite the talk of our social circle. There was a lot of speculation about the whole situation. So, to keep the record straight, I will tell you what happened, so you don't have to piece it together from gossip or hearsay."

Chapter 18

Rather taken aback by her frankness, Mike didn't comment, but just sat quietly, waiting for her to begin. Jana crossed her legs, wiggled a bit the chair, before, in a calm, well-modulated voice, her eyes connecting with his, she spoke. "From the very first time I met him, during our junior year at the University, I was captivated by James Browning. The first time I saw him was at a party after a football game; a large group had gathered in the student center and we wound up at the same table. There was a lively conversation about the game, mostly from the guys, who were discussing how our team had managed to salvage a win after being behind until right at the end of the fourth quarter. I was intrigued by his witty commentary on the coaching strategy. In contrast to most of the opinions offered by his friends, his criticism, although pointed, was not derogatory but politely offered options that could have been implemented. It was interesting; he was knowledgeable about the game. As I prepared to leave with my friends, he asked for my phone number. His call the next day ended with an invitation to dinner which I accepted. After that, we began dating, and that was that."

Mike noted how easily Jana relayed the information; she didn't hesitate, or search for words as she recalled the beginning of her relationship with the murdered man.

Without pausing, Jana continued, "We just clicked from the first date. We were both only children and both very close to our parents. He talked about his mother, recalling incidents from his childhood and teen years. I was shocked to learn she'd died shortly after he entered high school. When I started offering condolences, he stopped me by saying he had been blessed by her, and preferred to focus on the time they'd shared, rather than lamenting her loss.

To me, that statement revealed his outlook on life, and I was impressed. When he told me that his dad had passed away from cancer during his sophomore year in college, my heart went out to him. It was obvious to me that he was a strong, focused individual, looking forward to what life held, rather than becoming mired in the past."

Observing her as she talked, Mike was impressed with the information she offered; it gave insight to both her and James. That was rare. Most people being interviewed focused on themselves, trying to create a good impression, and they seldom offered anything but the most basic information.

Jana's next statement offered another facet of James Browning. She said, "He had many friends, but he could be somewhat of a loner, and I identified with him in that regard, because there were times when I, too, needed solitude from the demands of a busy college environment. He was laid back, very easy going, and always the first one to offer help to anyone who needed assistance."

As Mike listened to Jana, he was struck by how similar her description of James Browning was to what he'd heard from those who'd already been interviewed. He was beginning to think the guy was some sort of robot, programmed to follow a specific pattern. It was uncanny to him that no one, not even his ex-wife, offered a different opinion of him. It certainly didn't make sense that someone so congenial and nice as he was depicted, would be murdered. A foiled robbery was beginning to look more and more like the motive for what happened. He made no comment, waiting to hear what else Jana had to say.

Oblivious to Mike's speculations, Jana added, "Our relationship steadily developed. When he asked me to marry him, I was elated." For the first time since she'd begun speaking, she broke eye contact with Mike. He watched as she shifted about in the chair, seeming at a loss as how to continue. This wasn't the first time he'd heard talk about failed marriages, and he was well aware it could be difficult for the one recalling the events of the break-up. Always mindful that it could rekindle feelings of hurt, he was about to suggest they take a break, when Jana cleared her throat, and resumed talking.

There was no way he could have known, as she delivered her next words, that she was just parroting the practice interviews so carefully rehearsed in front of her bathroom mirror. Lowering her head, and briefly closing her eyes, she said very softly, "My wedding day was the happiest day of my life."

Her admission surprised Mike. To include that information, given how adamant she'd been about no longer having any connection to anything having to do with Browning, cast a different light on the woman sitting before him. Mentally, he gave her credit for the honesty about her feelings on her wedding day. In spite of her strong declarations about being done with him, it crossed his mind, as he noted the softness of her voice and heard her quiet words, that perhaps she still had feelings for the man who'd betrayed her.

As he observed her, it was almost as if she'd read his thought, she jerked her head upwards, abandoning any hint of fondness and reverted to her no nonsense tone, and continued, "We married in August after our graduation. Like most couples, we had plans and dreams. James had always wanted to be involved in some type of boating business; he loved the water and everything about it. Beginning his career as a salesman for a major boat builder was perfect for him. He was happy. I worked as an educational consultant for the junior college and enjoyed my job. We weren't wealthy by any means, but we didn't lack money. We had friends and a good life."

Chapter 19

Jana stopped for a moment, and then continued. "My parents died in a plane crash shortly after our first wedding anniversary. James, who completely understood the devastation and agony of losing parents, was my rock as I coped with all the things that had to be done, beginning with their funerals, and handling all the issues that had to be settled. I don't think I could have made it without him."

Again, Mike was struck by her willingness to give credit to her ex-husband. It was a direct contrast to the description he'd heard about her being a vindictive person fighting furiously to strip everything from him in the divorce settlement.

Jana didn't pause after that statement but shifted to another subject effortlessly. "When my parent's estate was settled, our financial position changed drastically. My inheritance eliminated all our money issues. After much discussion, we made the decision to start our own business. James was ecstatic and I was excited to see him realize his dream. We started Taking It Easy and worked together, creating a unique enterprise that is quite successful. It was a dream come true for James and seeing him so happy was special to me. In addition, it was quite profitable. Our life was full; we had a successful business and friends. We entertained often, took trips, and basically just enjoyed life. Plus, we had each other."

Mike had watched her intently as she spoke, noting her facial expressions, tone of voice, and body language. Except for the reference to her wedding day, and the acknowledgment of the support she'd received after the death of her parents, the information she'd offered had been straight-forward, without any emotion. It had been almost as if she was delivering a well-prepared speech.

He was about to ask her about how the subject of divorce had been broached when she said, "Detective, I've been talking for quite a while. I'd like to pause and get something to drink. Is that all right?"

"Of course," he replied. "We can take a break for a bit." She smiled, rising from the chair, and exiting the room.

While Jana was gone from the room, Mike and Jack chatted quietly, deliberately avoiding any discussion about the ongoing interview. Jack commented that the house was very nice, and Mike, who had already noted the beautiful decorations, agreed. When Jana returned to the room, bearing a tray with a pitcher and glasses filled with ice, she said, "I thought if I was thirsty, you probably were too, so I brought some lemonade." Pointing to a plate on the tray, she said, "These are homemade chocolate chip cookies, if you want them."

Jack chuckled and said, "This is the first time, I've ever been served refreshments by someone who was being interviewed." Mike nodded as he helped himself to a cookie, thinking Jana was indeed a unique person.

After the glasses were filled and distributed, Mike asked Jana how the subject of divorce first occurred. Carefully returning her lemonade to the tray, she looked at him, and said simply, "I was sitting at the breakfast table one Saturday morning, and James came in with a folder in his hands. When he said we needed to talk, I assumed there was something about the store we needed to discuss. Without warning, he told me he wanted a divorce, that our marriage was over, that he no longer loved me. He said he was moving out, that he'd rented an apartment. He opened the folder and pulled a document from it, handed me a pen, and said I needed to sign it."

"Wow," Jack said. "That must have been quite a shock."

She looked at both men for a moment before continuing, "There is no way to describe my feelings. Disbelief, shock, horror, all those words are appropriate, but they don't convey how I felt. I just sat there, staring at him, trying to make some sense out of what he'd said."

Mike noted that Jana's delivery of the information was flat, completely devoid of any emotion. Almost, as an afterthought, she added, "The funny thing is, I hadn't suspected anything. Never, in all the years we were together, did the thought our marriage would end, cross my mind. I was happy; I thought he was happy, but I was wrong. It was unbelievable to me that, after nineteen years, he didn't want me anymore."

"Did you sign the document he had for you?" Mike asked.

"I did not. I was in no shape to sign anything. He was very put out with me and spent several minutes trying to convince me to sign, but I just couldn't. Finally, he left the folder on the table, telling me he'd get it later, and stormed out of the room. After he left, I managed to call my friend, Shirley, who came over immediately. When I showed her the paper, she told me not to sign it, or anything else from him. She insisted I contact a lawyer."

She fixed her eyes on Mike, and added, in a very matter-of-fact voice, "The divorce was the most difficult thing I've ever experienced, even more difficult than the death of my parents. Coming to grips with the ending of my marriage and accepting that my life was nothing but a farce, took a long time. Later, learning about his affair was as painful as being told our marriage was over. My world was torn apart. My entire life had been centered on my husband and our business; the thought of continuing my life without him was unimaginable."

Chapter 20

She paused for a moment, retrieved her glass from the table, and after taking another sip of lemonade, said, "It took very in-depth counseling for me to finally realize our relationship was very one-sided, and that I'd been beyond naïve. Once reality dawned, overcoming the hurt, anger, and bitterness was quite a chore, but after much agony, I was able to go forward with my life."

Mike was surprised by her honesty and impressed with the way she described what must have been a devastating time in her life, in such a calm manner. He was also impressed by the lack of anger or hurt she'd shown relaying the information. Quietly he said, "I see," before clearing his throat and asking, "Was the divorce settlement easily reached?"

"No, it was not," she admitted. "Our lawyers worked long and hard to find an agreement that was acceptable to both of us." Mike watched Jana closely. She didn't appear upset, or angry, as she recounted dealing with the ending of her marriage.

"One thing became very clear to me as I began to cope with what was happening; I didn't spend years of my life building a business, putting my heart and soul into it, as well as a large part of my inheritance, to just step aside, and let James continue as if nothing had happened. Saying 'you go ahead and enjoy the fruits of our labors and I'll start over' wasn't possible." She paused for a moment before adding, "So no, the settlement was not easily reached. There wasn't anything pleasant about the negotiations. James was surprised that I didn't agree to everything he wanted, because that's the way it had always been, but I wasn't about to knuckle under to his demands. It was a long process, but eventually, we reached an agreement."

Her voice was quiet, well-modulated and almost flat as she spoke. It was apparent to Mike that the journey Jana Arnold had traveled had not been easy and that the end was reached only after much anguish. Scrutinizing her intensely, he could find no sign of anger, or hurt.

"How do you feel about your ex-husband?" he asked to further test her.

"I don't have any feelings about him," her quick answer was blunt, and matter of fact. "His betrayal almost killed me. I've had to learn to live my life completely separate from him, and the life we shared together. It took a good while, and although it was difficult, I've put it all behind me." Folding her hands together and placing them in her lap, she looked at Mike and said, "So now you know all about what happened. You might hear other things; everyone certainly had their own ideas about the divorce, but that's it in a nutshell."

Contemplating her response, Mike sat quietly. His gut feeling was that it had taken her a long time to accept and adjust to the ending of her marriage. She'd been straightforward in her statements; he had no reason to doubt the things she'd said. Jack looked expectantly across at him, but when he made no comment, he turned to Jana and said, "For the record, please tell us where you were on the day James was killed. Our asking you for that information in no way indicates you are under any suspicion, but we have to make a report, and it needs to be as complete as possible, which includes showing we've covered every base, and obtained all information that might have a bearing on the case."

Jana's response was light and easy as she offered, "That's a no-brainer. I spent the morning shopping at Grafton Department Store's big end of season sale. I think it was around 2:00 or so when I got home. I spent the rest of the afternoon preparing for a cook-out my friend, Shirley Lewis, and I were hosting for the children's theatre group we direct. Altogether, there were more than thirty people here."

Her willingness to answer erased any suspicion that she intended to withhold information about her whereabouts on the day of the incident. After a few more minutes the detectives ended the visit. As they were walking to the door, Jana said quietly, "I still can't believe James is dead. And for him to be murdered is beyond comprehension. I hope you are able to find out who is responsible."

After thanking her for talking with them, Mike and Jack bid her goodbye. She remained on the porch, watching them get into their car and drive away. As the vehicle made its way down the street, Jana took several deep breaths, and closed her eyes, satisfied she'd handled the visit well.

Chapter 21

During the drive back to the office, Mike and Jack discussed the interview with Jana. They talked about her beautiful home, especially its exquisite furnishing and immaculate yard, and then, almost as if he were thinking out loud, Jack said, "Jana Arnold is not at all what I expected. I can't say exactly what I was anticipating her to be like, but she doesn't fit into any category I've encountered before; she's certainly not the typical ex-wife."

Mike looked at his partner, surprised by his comments. Usually, Jack had no problem reaching conclusions about witnesses. He was a master at analyzing people; his careful scrutiny during interview sessions usually resulted in a complete personality overview. On the other hand, it took much longer for him to reach a conclusion about witnesses. Often, it was the inconsistencies in the overall picture that resulted in his opinion about someone. During their years of working together, the combination of the two approaches had been successful in determining the actual solution of puzzling cases.

Before he could comment, Jack continued, "She certainly offered a lot of information. I'm always suspicious when so many details are provided to general questions. And her description of events was almost too vivid; everything was described to a tee."

Nodding, Mike remarked, "From what I'd heard about her, I was expecting a very strict, stern, no nonsense person, one used to being completely in charge of everything. She really threw me for a loop when she brought us refreshments. Her whole attitude was different from what I expected. And, I do agree that she did elaborate more than necessary, but maybe, that's just the way she is about everything."

"Yeah, you have a point. That could be it," Jack answered, "but still, there were times I thought I was listening to a recording; everything was so flat and smooth. Not once did she pause, or search for words, or add an additional thought to her initial statement."

"She didn't struggle for words, that's for sure," Mike said, and then offered, "Her admission that she had a hard time accepting the fact Browning wanted a divorce, and how it took a long time for her to finally accept it, might explain the rote manner of her testimony."

As they pulled into the parking lot of the police station, Jack shook his head and observed. "Ms. Arnold is an interesting person, pleasant, friendly, and confident. I just can't get over how smooth and flawless her testimony was; it seemed rehearsed."

Mike responded, "Well, she's been very upfront about not having any idea a divorce was in her future, and the difficulty she had accepting it, as well as leaving no doubt how she feels about James Browning. Obviously, she's completely over him."

Shaking his head, Jack said, "I have my doubts about that. I think she harbors far more resentment than she wants anyone to see. She's too adamant about how counseling resolved all the issues surrounding the divorce. I understand how it could be helpful, but to say it solved everything is troubling, doesn't make sense, but maybe it's just me, and I'm dissecting her testimony too much. I keep thinking about the saying 'the guilty protests too much,'" Jack sighed as he retrieved his briefcase from the backseat.

"Trust your instinct, man," Mike said. "You've been doing this too long not to listen to it."

"I appreciate your confidence in me, but I've been off base before," Jack said good-naturedly, as they walked into the building and then added, "further investigation should settle any questions; more than likely it will supersede the manner her testimony was presented."

Chapter 22

Later that evening, as Mike sat on his patio enjoying a cup of coffee, his thoughts returned to the interview with Jana Arnold and the conversation he and Jack had afterward. Jack's evaluation that Jana Arnold had offered more than the usual amount of information in response to their routine questions was valid, definitely something to be considered. In his experience, those who supplied lengthy responses were usually trying to cover every issue that might have bearing on the situation in question. Also, false information was generally delivered either devoid of any emotion, or with carefully orchestrated tears, and excessive body language, to portray appropriate feelings.

Jana's presentation didn't really fit into either category. There had been no drama associated with her statements. Neither her tone of voice nor demeanor had fluctuated throughout her testimony, except when she admitted the happiest day of her life was the day she married. He remembered being surprised by the softness of her tone, and the expression on her face as she recounted that information. It had been completely out of sync with the rest of her hum-drum presentation. Also, the genuine gratitude she'd expressed when describing James's support when her parents died was another surprise. That acknowledgement revealed, that in spite of his betrayal, she had not forgotten his kindness.

Jana's direct, down-to-earth approach had presented a very straight-forward, factual overview of her relationship with James Browning, from beginning to end, which was exactly what she'd said she was going to do.

And, as Jack had mentioned, she had stressed that, without the extensive counseling guiding her, there was no way she would have ever gotten over the divorce. It made him wonder about the process she'd gone through and exactly what it entailed. As he continued mulling over her statement, he remembered a counselor from another case, several months ago, and how she'd been helpful in explaining the counseling steps used in it. Thoughtfully, he pulled his cell phone from his pocket, and, after consulting the contact list, punched in a number. Perhaps, he thought, it would be beneficial to learn more about how divorce counseling worked.

When Rachel Washington answered in a friendly voice, he announced, "It's Mike Stone, from Precinct 812; do you have a minute to talk?"

"Mike, it's been a long time," the voice replying was steady, and cordial. "To what do I owe this honor?"

Briefly, he explained his dilemma, adding "According to statements made, an extensive period of therapy helped the individual adjust to an unexpected divorce, and I am curious about what that type of counseling entails." He went on to outline his concern about the testimony, mentioning that precise details had been included, and that the manner in which they were presented seemed rehearsed, without any feeling or emotion. Summing up his concerns, he said, "On one hand, the details offer a wealth of information, but the manner in which they were relayed is puzzling. Much emphasis was given to how the counseling was the reason the divorce was accepted, allowing the person to begin a new life, but somehow, the presentation of the statement is troubling. So, I am wondering how counseling works in situations like this."

Rachel's response was thorough, and straightforward. "Although I don't know the specifics of this case, I can say, getting someone to accept their spouse wants a divorce can be very difficult. It often involves going through a step-by-step process of analyzing the marriage, from beginning to end, in an effort to identify events that led to its failure. The purpose of doing that is to point out indicators that the relationship was unstable. Seemingly unimportant events can actually be red flags, but recognition of negative factors in the relationship doesn't always happen quickly," she offered. "Admitting that significant warning signs were missed is difficult;

most individuals do not dwell on their failure to recognize the signs along the way. Often, a person will pretend to acknowledge them, but in reality, will cast them aside, denying their importance, and just eventually, pretending to understand. If that's the case, an unemotional presentation makes sense."

After chatting for a few more minutes, Mike thanked Rachel for her help and ended the call. Drumming his fingers on the table beside his chair, Mike reviewed Rachel's information. Taking into consideration Jana's explanation of how extensive her therapy had been, it seemed plausible that the recognition and acceptance of her flawed marriage was the result of going through the steps Rachel described, and finally, just accepting that the divorce was unavoidable. That might explain her unemotional presentation. It also made Jack's speculation that she wasn't really over the divorce plausible.

"Time will tell," he muttered to himself, as he went back into the house and placed his cup in the sink.

The following week, Jack Beatty had an emergency appendectomy, and the James Browning murder case became Mike's sole responsibility. He declined having another detective assigned to help him, saying he could handle the current case alone until Jack was able to return to duty. Because his reputation in the department was flawless, his boss agreed. So alone, Mike Stone continued the tedious task of investigating the murder of James Browning.

Chapter 23

It had been over twenty years since the police department re-organized its detective department, creating teams to handle homicide investigations. At the time it occurred, Mike questioned the change, thinking it was a waste to assign two officers to one case, but it didn't take him long to recognize the wisdom of the decision. It became quickly apparent that when a pair of detectives worked together conducting interviews, examining evidence, and reviewing collected data, the chance of missing key factors was greatly reduced. It was almost uncanny, how, when there were two people working a case, the details one person failed to see, the other noticed; working a case alone presented challenges having a partner alleviated. The most obvious benefit was having someone carefully observe people involved in the investigation, noting facial expressions, or body language and the overall general demeanor that a person concentrating on documenting conversations missed. Those non-verbal reactions often supplied significant insight to the validity of what was being said. Even the tiniest fact could be important.

Also, not having Jack work with him presented the possibility that some information might be disregarded or forgotten in the investigation process. To eliminate that happening, the first thing Mike did was create a written summary of everything he knew about James Browning and his murder, beginning with his and Jack's initial visit to the crime scene. He also put together a detailed chart of interviews. Reviewing the sparseness of the completed project, he had to acknowledge there wasn't much to go on, but he was confident that with careful investigating, this case, like all the others he'd worked on, could be solved.

Carefully reviewing all the comments that had been made about the man, Mike couldn't help thinking that James Browning must have been a rather boring individual. There was nothing special about him, according to the information he'd gathered; the consensus was that he was just an all-around good guy, an average Joe who didn't have any enemies. But the fact that James Browning had been murdered so callously contradicted that conclusion.

So far, the only person raising any suspicion was his ex-wife, Jana Arnold, but there was no evidence against her yet. The interview with her had raised no red flags; all questions had been answered willingly with no apparent hesitancy on her part. His gut feeling was that she'd had nothing to do with the murder, but the logical course of action was to continue the investigation until either her guilt or innocence was confirmed.

Musing over the files, Mike considered his options. Three things, two of which might offer some insight to Jana Arnold's involvement in Browning's demise, and one that was crucial to her involvement, stood out as he reviewed the information. Interviewing Shirley Lewis, Jana's friend, could provide Jana's reaction to learning of Browning's murder, as well as insight to the couple's marriage. The particulars of the divorce settlement would provide information regarding the effect his death would have on Jana and verifying her visit to the department store at the time of Browning's murder would solidify her alibi. Confident he was on the right track, Mike planned his course of action.

It was really too late in the day to pursue any of the tasks, but after a quick review of his notes, he found Shirley Lewis's phone number and punched it into his cell phone. In a few minutes, an interview was scheduled. Sighing, he gathered all his notes and placed them in the folder assigned to the case.

Chapter 24

Entering the conference room the next morning, Mike was surprised that the woman sitting at the conference table was not at all what he'd expected; he'd assumed Jana Arnold's friend would be as stylish and attractive as she was, but that was not the case. Older, and rather frumpy, she was the opposite of Jana. Her discomfort was apparent as she gazed awkwardly around the room.

"Good morning," he said pleasantly, extending his hand toward her. "I'm Mike Stone, the investigator who spoke with you yesterday. Thank you for coming in."

"Hello," the woman answered, "I'm Shirley Lewis."

"You are probably wondering why you were asked to come in," Mike offered. "Let me put your mind at ease. Whenever an incident such as the death of James Browning occurs, we contact as many people we can who knew the victim, hoping we may discover something that will help in the investigation. Ms. Arnold told us you were the one who told her about James's death and that you were her best friend who had known Mr. Browning for some time."

Shirley nodded in agreement to his statement but offered no other response.

"Please understand that in no way does asking for your input suggest that you or Ms. Arnold are implicated in the crime. Investigations require that all people with ties to the deceased person be contacted to gather information that might have some impact on what happened," Mike continued in a friendly tone of voice.

Since Jack was not with him to catch any subtleties, Mike focused his attention wholly on Shirley to monitor her reactions or any change in her behavior that might offer more than the words she spoke. His careful observation noted how her friendly expression suddenly became guarded and how her eyes immediately shifted from this face as she began concentrating on the folded hands in her lap.

Continuing to watch her carefully, Mike kept his expression non-committal and congenial. "Tell me about your relationship with the Brownings. I know you've been friends for many years."

"I've known Jana since we were kids, and I met James while we were in college, shortly after he and Jana began dating," she said.

"What sort of person was he? Did you see him often?" Mike asked.

Hesitantly, Shirley began speaking. Without any emotion, she replied, "I'd listened to Jana talking about him for weeks, and from her comments, I thought he'd be fantastic; but, to be honest, he didn't impress me at all the first time I met him. I couldn't see why Jana was taken with him." Pausing a moment, she sighed and then said, "Jana was in love with him from the moment they met, always doing everything he wanted, putting aside anything she preferred, and going along with his ideas."

"How would you describe him?" Mike asked.

She raised her head, and with her eyes unwavering, stated bluntly, "He wasn't my favorite person; Jana is like a sister to me and I wanted the best for her. I doubt my expectations were reasonable, but anyone would have pleased me more than James did."

"So, what was it about him that you didn't like? Was he dishonest, or mean; how would you sum him up?" Mike prodded.

For the next few minutes, Shirley Lewis talked about her feelings for James Browning. She had nothing positive to say about him. Straightforward, she told of watching the relationship between Jana and Browning grow; she said that she was Jana's maid of honor in their wedding and, that through the years, she and her husband had maintained close to the couple, going on trips together and being in one another's homes. But her overall assessment of James Browning was negative; most of her comments were unflattering. She very candidly offered her opinion that having Taking It Easy let him avoid work and escape the responsibility required by a real job.

Her analysis of him was that Jana's inheritance and business savvy had enabled him to be an honorable bum, spending time piddling with boats, instead of actually tending to business matters. "He is, was, self-centered and spoiled in my opinion," she stated flatly.

"I see," Mike responded. "Was there friction between him and his wife? Did his actions aggravate her in any way you could see?" he asked, wondering if Jana Arnold had become disenchanted with her lazy husband.

"No, Jana refused to be realistic about him. She made excuses, emphasizing his talent working with boats. My husband told me to accept him for the sake of my friendship with Jana and that's what I did."

Seeing that her statements had been upsetting, Mike said, "Let's take a break. We need to stretch our legs. The rest room is at the end of the hall. I'll get us some drinks from the machine."

Shirley nodded her head and cast him a grateful look as she got up from the table. He watched as she walked away, thinking that perhaps she'd understood Browning better than anyone.

Chapter 25

When Shirley returned, Mike said, "I appreciate your candidness. We're almost finished. I know it can be difficult to talk about friends but having information from more than one person helps clear up the fuzzy things that are concerning."

Shirley didn't answer, but the look on her face was more peaceful than it had been. When Mike asked about the Browning's marriage, she said that Jana was completely besotted by James. When talking about the divorce, her voice broke, recalling how for a time, Jana was completely at a loss.

"She became a totally different person during that time," Shirley relayed, "unable to make decisions, and losing focus on things that needed to be done. For the first time ever, she was frightened to stay alone; she was not sleeping or eating properly. It was very painful to see her that way. My heart ached for her. When she confided how scared she was at night, I convinced her to go with me to the gun shop over on Fourth Street, buy a gun and take their self-defense course. At first, she didn't want to go, but I persuaded her by insisting I wanted to get a permit and didn't want to do it alone. We took the course together, and it seemed to help Jana overcome her fear."

As Mike listened patiently, he was impressed by the woman sitting before him. Shirley spoke frankly, with simple honesty; she didn't try to hide her misgivings about James Browning or how his betrayal had devastated Jana. She said it had taken Jana a long time to get past the anger and hurt it caused, adding "Jana finally snapped out of the depression that had overtaken her when she became aware that James was trying to take their business from her. She had worked to make it successful and she was so proud of it. It was what made her address the situation," she added. "Fighting for Taking it

Easy and extensive counseling permitted her to make a new life for herself."

When Shirley paused, Mike took the opportunity to ask, "You were the one who told Jana about James's death?"

"Yes, I was. When I learned from television news what happened to him, I knew I needed to get to her as soon as possible. We were hosting a party for the youth drama club we sponsor so there were already plans to be at her house. I was hoping she hadn't heard about it."

"And she didn't know until you told her?" Mike asked.

"No, she said she had been busy preparing for the party and hadn't turned on the television. My concern was that his dying might trigger new emotional trauma for her, but thank goodness, it didn't. She was very matter of fact that any connection between the two of them was gone. We discussed whether she should attend his funeral, but she said she needed to think about it. The next morning, she called, and, in true Jana fashion, she said she'd decided her being there would just rekindle gossip, so she was not going. She did say she wanted to honor their time together in some way and asked what I thought about her gathering a bouquet of roses from their garden and tossing them from the bridge into the waters of the lake."

At Mike's quizzical look, she explained, "The roses were special; soon after they married, James created the rose garden, picking different varieties of plants and arranging them strategically to create a beautiful array of color. It was a beautiful place to just go sit and smell the fragrance of the blooms and feast your eyes on the color spectacle. Jana always said it was their favorite place to eat dinner. When she mentioned taking some to the lake, which was also another one of their special places, and throwing them out onto the water, I wholehearted agreed with her proposal. It was something private she could do that would acknowledge the happiness they once shared. It was evident to me she's put the whole ordeal in proper perspective. Jana's a wonderful, kind individual," Shirley confided to Mike, "who just fell in love with the wrong person. He never deserved her."

They talked for a few more minutes, and after expressing his thanks for her meeting with him, Mike escorted Shirley to the elevator ending the interview. Making his way to his desk, he reviewed the things that had been discussed, concluding how Shirley Lewis had confirmed Jana Arnold's statement about the divorce being a long ordeal, and that the adjustment had been very difficult for her. It was interesting that Jana's best friend's opinion of James Browning, unlike that of everyone else he'd spoken to, was not at all favorable. It had been an interesting encounter, but he had to admit it contained nothing useful toward solving the murder.

Chapter 26

Once back at his desk, Mike carefully entered notes about Shirley Lewis's interview into the case file. Sighing as the task was finished, Mike rolled his chair back from his desk and gazed out the window, letting his thoughts wander. Niggling bits of information kept running through his mind as he considered everything he knew about James Browning's murder. So far, the only person raising any suspicion was his ex-wife, Jana Arnold, but, the information that had been gathered didn't offer any real evidence against her.

His thoughts wandered to the next item on his list of things to investigate. The many statements that the Browning's divorce proceedings had been long and hard fought, a battle which Jana had pursued relentlessly, couldn't be used to accuse her of murder, but neither could they be ignored. To her credit, Jana Arnold herself had been very straightforward about the conflict, not hiding how it had taken a long time to reach an agreement. She'd readily admitted that learning James Browning wanted sole ownership of their business had been the impetus that made her stand up and fight what he proposed. Thinking about how she'd freely offered that information, without any hesitation or excuses, Mike acknowledged he hadn't found her position unusual; it was reasonable that anyone would oppose losing something that had taken so much time, money and effort. He knew from handling other cases, that divorce proceedings could be brutal; the fact the couple had battled over theirs wasn't really significant. However, it might provide some insight to why James was no longer in the picture. Scanning through the file, he located the name of the attorney who'd represented Jana in the proceedings.

Later that afternoon, Mike was in the office of Jake Asher, the lawyer who'd handled Jana's divorce. An older man with an outstanding reputation, Asher was cordial, but also very direct, stating that, other than confirming he was Jana's attorney, he wasn't prepared to offer any other information about her or the divorce.

In an effort to east the situation, smiling, Mike said, "I've spoken to Ms. Arnold at length; and she told me that the proceedings were long and drawn out because she'd been determined to retain a share of the business. To complete my file, I need to document the specifications of the settlement."

It was obvious to Mike that neither his friendly demeanor nor his need for facts about the divorce impressed Jake. He was not persuaded to change his stance on disclosing information. Speaking firmly, Jake said, "I understand your interest, but you need to know my dealings with clients are confidential. I cannot share anything with you without their consent. I will contact Ms. Arnold and tell her you are requesting specifics of the suit. Perhaps she will give her permission for me to talk to you."

Recognizing that Jake was not going to divulge anything until he was given permission, Mike nodded and responded, "I'd appreciate that. I'm sure Ms. Arnold will consent."

Leaning forward, Jake pressed the intercom button on his desk, and asked his secretary to get Jana on the phone. In a few minutes, after ending a brief conversation, he addressed Mike stating, "Jana has given me permission to share the details of the settlement with you." For the first time, his tone was friendly as he commented, "You must have impressed her; it's not like her to let anyone know about her business. She said I should feel free to answer any questions."

Mike nodded, replying, "She does seem to be an unusual person; she has been very forthcoming about her relationship with James Browning. All questions have been answered willingly, without hesitation."

The attorney looked at Mike thoughtfully, "That would be Jana. She's always responded appropriately whatever the situation, being the one who gave far more than was expected. In my opinion, she certainly did that in her marriage. She wanted to be the perfect wife. The saddest part of it all is that I think, she still, to this day, loves that scoundrel."

Jake, a reflective expression on his face, paused for a moment, and then said, "Her Dad and I were friends for years. I watched Jana grow up; she was her daddy's pride and joy. Excelling in everything she did, she was almost a carbon copy of him. When she met James Browning, she fell hook, line, and sinker. I was never impressed with him, and neither was her dad, but there was no convincing her James wasn't Prince Charming."

Mike nodded. Jake's statement corroborated what Shirley Lewis had said. "That's what I've gathered from talking to her friends," he agreed.

"When we first met concerning the divorce, I couldn't believe how much she'd changed. After the death of her parents, I handled all the legal matters surrounding their estate and we saw each other often, but we'd had very little contact after that. When she came to my office, she was in a horrible state, her appearance was startling, almost unkempt, not like her at all. She was confused, hurt, angry and alone. Without her best friend, Shirley, I don't know what have happened to her." He paused, obviously recalling the difference in Jana's appearance. When he began speaking again, his tone was steely. Adamantly he stated, "I'll tell you one thing; if her Dad had still been alive, he would have eliminated James Browning. He was the type of man who didn't tolerate betrayal of any sort; his standards were set in stone. His mantra was "Do what is right, don't tolerate anything less. I'm glad he wasn't here; it would not have been pretty."

Chapter 27

Hearing this, for the first time Mike thought about Jana's predicament in a different light. Perhaps being the one who was betrayed had affected her more because of her father's influence. He offered a comment, "Everyone I've talked to has mentioned that Jana fought long and hard to get what she wanted. James's friends all agree that he finally gave in because she was relentless throughout the proceedings. What did she want from the agreement?" he asked.

The older gentleman paused for a moment, and then began talking. "It was most unusual," he offered. "I'd never had that type of settlement before. In my opinion, it came about because basically, Jana was so determined to retain an interest in the business. It took weeks for the details to be worked out. I think James finally agreed to her demands just to get the whole thing over with; he was tired of dragging it on, and he wanted to be free to marry again." A look of contempt crossed his face as he offered, "And he never was one for sticking to anything; he always wanted an easy way out."

"What was finally decided?" Mike asked.

"There were three options; the business could be sold; one could buy out the other or it could be sold commercially; they could continue operating the business as before, with Jana managing the store and James operating the Boat Rental section, or one of them could operate it and pay the other. Neither of them wanted to sell – both stated they didn't want to buy the other out, and because real estate prices in that area continued to sky-rocket it would be foolish to sell commercially at that time. Finally, after much discussion, an agreement was reached that Browning would assume responsibility for the daily business operation. Although he wanted Jana to continue running the store, she was not willing to do so, much to his irritation."

Mike recalled Jana's statements about not wanting to be involved in the daily operations. He inquired, "How did they settle the financial aspect?"

"They had to reach an agreement about the financial matters. It was complicated process. Jana finally agreed that in lieu of alimony, she'd accept a percentage of the business's profits, which would be paid quarterly. It was a good deal for James, because a set alimony fee did not account for fluctuations in the business profits."

"Wasn't that a concession on her part," Mike asked.

"Actually, it was a pretty shrewd move, although it was a gamble of sorts. The profits had steadily increased and there was no reason to think the trend would not continue, so it was a good bet she would receive more than a set sum based on the current intake. James did not have a problem with it.

"However, the most bizarre aspect of the settlement was that they would continue joint ownership of both the business and the property. They also agreed that upon the death of either of them, the business and the property would go to the surviving one. Jana kept reminding James it was her inheritance that had enabled them to establish the business and that both of them had worked hard to make it what it was. She kept stressing how it was the fair and right thing to do for both of them. Not addressed was how important to her that Mr. Browning's new wife would not, in the event James died, inherit the business. And James, being James, wasn't really concerned about the long-term future. Although I don't know it for a fact, he probably thought everything would be sold long before he died."

"So, Ms. Arnold receives payments from the business, but she is not involved in the daily operation?" Mike asked.

"That's correct," Jake answered, "she's paid based on the profits for each quarter."

A spark of interest igniting in his brain he asked, "And James Browning's death benefits her even more?"

Jake Asher looked at Mike with unwavering eyes, "Yes, since James died, she will become sole owner of both the business and the property."

The news was stunning. It put a whole new spin on James's murder, once again stirring up suspicions about Jana Arnold. The two men chatted for a few more minutes before Mike stood up and extended his hand to Jake, saying, "Thank you, you have been most helpful."

Chapter 28

Checking his watch as he exited the attorney's office, and noting it was too late in the day to visit Grafton's Department store, Mike decided the review of the surveillance tapes would be the first thing on tomorrow's agenda. Stopping at his office, he answered a couple of random messages and updated the Browning case file records before heading home.

A quick dinner of left-over spaghetti didn't take long, and neither did putting the kitchen back in order. When satisfied with the way things looked, Mike filled a big insulated mug with freshly-brewed coffee and ventured out to the patio and, as usual, settled in the huge padded chair he'd claimed as his years before. Relaxing in its comfortable cushions, his feet propped up on the ottoman and enjoying the soothing flavor of his favorite beverage had become a daily ritual after the death of his wife. At first, coming home to an empty house had been excruciating. She'd always been there, so happy to see him, with dinner ready and eager to share the events of her day and listen to his. Without her, he'd been lost, wandering aimlessly through the quiet rooms, trying to find a way to fill the void her absence created. Overcome with being by himself in the space they'd once shared, loneliness had engulfed him, making it impossible to concentrate. His thoughts had been consumed with the reality that she'd never return and thinking about anything else had been out of the question.

It had been quite by chance that, one evening, he'd taken a cup of coffee outside and sank into the deep cushions of the big chair. Somehow, it had felt right, and soon, a new routine was established. Ending his day outside was different; it gave him a chance to unwind and put things in order in a setting different from the one he'd shared with his wife. He loved the quietness that surrounded the arrival of twilight and watching the sun sink slowly out of sight.

Sipping the coffee, he admitted to himself that the Browning case was frustrating. Despite the detailed investigation of the crime scene and many interviews with various people, nothing significant had surfaced. While there was some interest in the ex-wife, no evidence linked her to the murder. Jana Arnold had willingly cooperated with the authorities. She'd answered questions and offered her whereabouts on the day of the crime without hesitation. In his opinion she had been truthful. He fully expected her alibi to be validated by the Grafton store tapes. Admittedly, her presentation had been somewhat stilted, but it needed to be noted that she'd been sharing information about her troubled marriage that had surely been painful to disclose. Through it all, she'd been pleasant; he smiled thinking how she'd brought lemonade to him and Jack.

But today's revelation from her attorney cast a new light on the situation; the fact that, as a result of James Browning's death, she alone would inherit the property and the business, put a new slant on the case; it presented a motive that had to be investigated thoroughly. Mike was reminded again of the remark James's friend made about Jana hiring someone to murder him. As darkness folded over him, Mike drained the last of the coffee from his mug, pushed the Browning case out of his mind, and went into the house, ready to watch the baseball game on TV.

Chapter 29

The next morning, when Mike arrived at the department store, he was ushered into a small office where the young manager of Grafton's greeted him warmly. "How can I help you?" he asked after they'd chatted for a brief moment.

"I need to review all the surveillance film from the first day of your annual sale," Mike replied, adding, "It might contain information about one of our cases."

"That's no problem. We have three different cameras recording store activity; one at the entrance captures customers coming and going; another, mounted in the ceiling of the store center, makes sweeping surveys of all areas, and another records check-out counter activity. We keep the tapes for 90 days and then forward them to our corporate headquarters. Give me a minute to get the ones you want. Will you view them here or take them with you?" he asked.

"I'll look at them here, and if I need to take them to the station, I will let you know," Mike replied.

The manager nodded and made a quick call. It wasn't long before a clerk appeared with a laptop. "The tapes from all three cameras are loaded and ready to view," he said, placing the apparatus on the desk. "Let me know if you need anything."

Mike thanked him and pressed 'start.' Almost immediately, he spotted Jana Arnold removing her sunglasses and placing them in her handbag. Noting the bright red skirt and checkered blouse she was wearing, Mike smiled, thinking she certainly wouldn't be hard to track in that outfit. As she walked into the store, the time in the upper right-hand corner of the film read 10:15 a.m. There was no other record of her on that film until 1:30 p.m. as she left the store.

Film from the camera that continually rotated throughout the store didn't focus on any one area for more than a few seconds. Only fleeting glimpses of individuals were captured. At one point, because of her bright red skirt, Mike was able to identify Jana entering the dressing room section. Her exit was not captured. Quite a bit later, she was briefly visible in the home goods section, putting items in a shopping cart.

The video from the checkout area presented better documentation. A smiling Jana could clearly be seen removing items from a shopping cart and placing them onto the counter. It recorded the cashier as she scanned price tags on the items and placed them in bags. After the last item was bagged, it showed Jana handing something, presumably a credit card, to her then taking a piece of paper, probably a receipt, along with the shopping bags and leaving the store.

Wanting to be absolutely sure he hadn't missed anything, Mike re-ran the tape from the entrance camera again to confirm Jana had not, at some point, left the store and then returned. Because of the sale, activity around the door was brisk; many customers were entering and leaving. Watching the film, Mike found it interesting, that women, unlike men, shopped in groups. It wasn't uncommon to see three or four women arriving together. It was ironic to him; he could not recall a single time when he'd shopped with a group of men. As far as he was concerned, shopping was a necessity, not a social outing. But, it was obvious the women at the Grafton's sale did not share his view; they were laughing and talking and obviously enjoying their time together. He was also struck by how similar many of them looked: their bobbed hairstyles and clothing selections, mostly long t-shirts over tight fitting pants, didn't vary much at all. As the tape ended, Mike sighed, acknowledging his careful scrutiny had found no image of Jana Arnold in her bright red outfit exiting and re-entering the store between the 10:14 and 1:30 times, just as her testimony stated.

Chapter 30

Mike pressed the 'off' button on the laptop, pushed the chair back from the table, and contemplated what he'd just seen. He was satisfied Jana Arnold's whereabouts on the day of the crime had been appropriately verified. Although it wasn't really necessary to do so, Mike decided to go the extra step and review the store credit card purchase records. Scanning through copies of the transactions quickly revealed that Ms. Arnold's American Express card had been used at 1:22 p.m. supplying additional confirmation to her claim that she had been at Grafton's.

Ever the meticulous detective, after leaving the department store, Mike went to the shopping center security center to check out the video of the parking lot. After showing his badge, he was ushered into a small conference room outfitted with several big television-type screens where an employee monitored a video of the current parking lot activity. Mike showed his credentials to another officer and furnished the date and area he needed to review. In a few minutes, the appropriate film cartridge was loaded into a monitor and Mike found himself watching the image of Jana's vehicle cruising slowly down the lanes of the parking lot. It stopped and waited as a car pulled out of a space, and then parked in the vacated slot. Jana, in her bright red skirt, was clearly visible getting out of the car and heading toward Grafton's. Locking the tape to focus on Jana's car, the clerk fast-forwarded it until Jana re-appeared at 1:33 p.m., got in and drove away. There was no doubt the vehicle had not been moved since it was put there at 10:12 that morning. After expressing his appreciation to the officer, Mike headed back to the police station.

As he updated the case file, Mike painstakingly analyzed the facts the morning's efforts had uncovered. All evidence supported

Jana's explanation that she'd been at Grafton's annual sale during the time of the murder; her alibi was airtight. Any suspicion that she had been the one to end James Browning's life at Taking It Easy had been effectively squelched. For all practical purposes, no further investigation of her was necessary, but although it made no sense whatsoever, Mike couldn't put Jana Arnold out of his mind. There was no plausible explanation to continue investigating her, but there was no denying the fact he felt compelled to do so.

Idly considering the reasons that might be responsible for his feelings, Mike had to admit Jana Arnold was a very interesting person. She was a direct, pull-no-punches sort of individual and from the very first, he had been impressed by the way she dealt with being questioned, never hesitating to offer answers and explanations. However, sometimes, a vague feeling that something wasn't right washed over him. It had never been anything in particular, just an uneasiness he couldn't explain. Maybe that was why he wanted to be sure there were no loose ends to be speculated about; he just didn't know.

Toying with his pencil, he tried to find the reason he wanted to keep investigating. Perhaps it was his partner's initial intuition about her that made him extra cautious. However, Jack's concern had centered on the manner in which Jana had relayed her testimony, but her stilted presentation had been effectively explained by the counselor Mike consulted. Or, maybe it was the comment from the coffee shop owner who'd laughingly said Jana would have been a good suspect if the murder had occurred during the divorce proceedings. It had opened a whole can of worms, but both Jana and her friend, Shirley, had explained the statement that she'd rather see Browning dead than married to someone else was merely Jana's way of expressing how hurt she was over the ending of her marriage. Mike could certainly understand how the declaration might just have been a desperate attempt to explain her hurt and anger over having her husband cast her aside for someone else. In addition, the information that Jana had purchased a gun and taken lessons to learn how to shoot it was troubling. But it was also reasonable to think it had been done for her own preservation, not the ending of someone else's life.

The new information that she would inherit the business and property did add a disturbing factor, even though there was rock-solid evidence supporting her innocence. However, there was the remote possibility that Jana could have hired someone to kill her ex-husband. She might be in a position where she needed the money and had decided it was time to claim what was really hers. In order to do so, James had to be eliminated. It was the remaining theory that needed to be addressed and until it was resolved, the case against Jana couldn't be closed. Mike breathed a sigh of relief to find a reason for his feelings. It was time for another visit to Ms. Arnold. Determined, he reached for the phone.

Chapter 31

Jana was not really surprised when Mike Stone called. After identifying himself, he asked if it was convenient for him to stop by and visit with her for a few minutes.

"Whatever for?" she asked. "I thought we covered everything the last time we talked."

"For the most part we did," he said, "and I apologize for having to bother you again, but there are a couple of issues we didn't cover that I need to include in my investigation. It won't take long at all, I promise."

"I am at home and don't have any appointments," she replied. "You can come now, if you want."

As she hung up the phone, her mind explored the possible reasons he wanted to talk to her again. Most probably, it was the divorce settlement that warranted further conversation. It made sense the detective would want to talk to her since his visit with her attorney who, she was sure, told him she was set to inherit the business and the property. There would probably be questions about her financial status to rule out any suggestion the inheritance was the cause of James's murder. She was fully prepared to address the fact that she had no need for money.

After spending a few minutes checking her make-up, applying her favorite cologne, and running a brush through her hair, she put on a fresh pot of coffee and sliced the banana bread she'd baked that morning. When the doorbell rang, she answered promptly, giving the detective a welcoming smile as she extended her hand in greeting.

"Thank you for seeing me, Ms. Arnold," Mike said as they shook hands. "I promise I won't take much of your time."

"Please call me Jana," she responded pleasantly, motioning for him to come in before saying, "Let's go to the kitchen. I have fresh coffee and banana bread just out of the oven. Surely, you'll take time to enjoy some of each."

A bit taken aback, Mike said whole-heartedly, "Well, I won't refuse that offer!" Following her through the house, once again Mike noted how inviting it was. The furniture, artwork, and accessories blended perfectly, creating a comfortable, peaceful setting. There were even fresh flowers in an exquisite vase on the table in front of the couch. A delicious aroma of freshly-baked bread filled the air when they entered the kitchen, reminding Mike of days passed when he'd been greeted by similar fragrances as he'd arrived home from a long day's work. After settling in the chair Jana indicated, he said, "You have a beautiful home."

Obviously surprised by his comment, Jana replied, "Thank you. My parents gave me this house the summer before I married. Honestly, I think Dad worried that James would have me living in some low-rent apartment project," she chuckled as she poured coffee into two mugs on the table; she put generous slices of banana bread on the plates beside them. "Mother and I spent hours and hours shopping for furniture and everything else a house needs and even more hours decorating it."

Observing her closely, Mike noted the information was offered simply, in a matter-of-fact manner. Not noticing his scrutiny, Jana continued easily, "It looks very different now from how it looked then. Thanks to my friend Shirley, it underwent a complete remodel after the divorce. At first, I rejected the idea, but she kept prodding me until I relented. Admittedly, it was wise to create new surroundings," she confided, sitting down in the chair across the table from Mike. "Since everything else in my life had changed, it made no sense to hang onto an environment filled with meaningless memories." She smiled, before adding, "I understand James had a new place built on the other side of the city; I've never seen it but the gossip is that it makes this place look small and out of date."

Mike found her comments a bit startling, to the point and refreshingly honest. It crossed his mind that Jana herself fit that category. In every interview, she'd been direct, offering information willingly and usually devoid of emotion, except for an occasional sprinkle of humor. Before he could say anything, Jana changed the subject completely, asking "What brings you here today, Detective?"

Mike paused a moment before answering. He wanted to assure Jana, and himself, that his visit was necessary to get clarification on some issues. Deciding that being straightforward was the best way to handle Jana Arnold, he took a deep breath and began. "The particulars of your divorce settlement are most unusual and suggest the possibility there might be further disputes involving adherence to them," he said, hastily adding, "I apologize if it is a painful subject, but every detail needs to be documented."

Chapter 32

Jana looked at him, not confirming nor denying her feelings regarding the request. Her voice firm, she replied, "Let me explain. Since I did not want to deal with James, or the business, the divorce agreement specified that if there was any problem or concern about the day-to-day operation or the property, Mr. Asher, my attorney, would be contacted to handle the issue. Of course, I am to be kept informed of any major irregularities, but the day-to-day decisions are made without my input. James was never to contact me. To date, nothing has needed my attention."

As Mike observed the attractive woman sitting across from him, he silently chided himself for pursuing the investigation. There was nothing to suggest she was behind her ex-husband's murder; he was wasting time, both his and hers, and for the life of him he didn't know why. Still attempting to justify his visit, his next statement was aimed at obtaining additional information about the relationship between her and her ex-husband during the divorce proceedings, perhaps uncovering something that had escalated animosity between them. To demonstrate a professional, business atmosphere, he cleared his throat before continuing in a rather know-it-all tone, "I see. That's a bit unusual, isn't it?" He watched her carefully, hoping her answer would give him some new avenue to investigate.

Jana looked at him quizzically for a moment before a mischievous smile spread across her face. Eyes twinkling, she said primly, "Well, I've only been involved in one divorce; I don't know what is usual."

Caught completely off guard by her teasing reply, Mike threw back his head and laughed. "Touché'! You made your point; I withdraw my question!" He took a bite of the banana bread, silently acknowledging to himself his clever attempt at securing additional information had failed.

Suddenly abandoning her frivolous, playful attitude, Jana became serious, and asked directly, "So what's the real reason you are here?

Side-stepping her question, Mike said easily, "Tell me about the business, how's it going now, since the death of James?"

"I don't really know. As I told you, my attorney is in charge of all the aspects of the financial matters involving Taking It Easy. I trust him to handle everything. I expect, in view of the recent happenings, I'll be contacted soon but I have no idea how the next step will be completed," Jana answered calmly.

"Do you know how much the business is worth?" he asked.

Shaking her head, Jana answered, "No, I do not. In years past, at any given moment, I could have quoted its value down to the penny, but that was when the business was so much a part of my life. I lived and breathed every aspect of that store; it was my baby." As she spoke those words, her whole demeanor changed. Her head dropped ever so slightly, her voice became subdued, and there was an air of helplessness about her that he'd never witnessed before. Very quietly, she said, "The divorce changed everything for me; what I'd valued and cherished suddenly became meaningless; the one person I'd loved and leaned on, and trusted, didn't want me anymore. I was nothing. I had no use. There was no reason for me to go on. The anguish from losing my husband and all that goes with that relationship would have been unbearable enough alone, but I also lost a business which was the center of my life—one I'd sunk my heart and soul into for years. In one instant, with a simple statement, life as I knew it was completely taken away; suddenly, my entire identity was destroyed. It was frightening, humiliating, and agonizing."

As Mike listened, for the first time the toll the divorce had taken on her was obvious, and he tried to imagine what it had been like when her world collapsed. He could identify with the situation somewhat; the tremendous loss when his wife died had been overwhelming, but that had been different from Jana's situation. Neither he nor his wife had instigated or had control over what was happening; their love for each other had remained strong throughout the entire time.

As Jana bared the hurt she'd experienced when her marriage ended, sympathy flooded through him. Having the one you loved betray you like Browning had betrayed her was out of his realm of comprehension, but it was clear that, although she had survived and accepted her fate, she would forever be affected by what had happened. For the very first time since he'd met her, she'd allowed a glimpse of the devastation the ending of her marriage had caused her. All the prior explanations had been factual, but none had included the emotion evident in today's revelation. She deserved to be commended for her determination to make a new life.

Chapter 33

A deafening silence hung in the air; Jana sat silently with her head bowed low, almost as if in a trance, and Mike, his attention completely focused on her, uttered not a word. Finally, breaking the spell, Jana raised her head and said briskly, "I'm sorry; you didn't ask about me; you asked about the business." Once again in control, she gazed at Mike unwaveringly, trying to decide what to say next.

Not wanting to interrupt her, Mike made no comment, waiting for her to continue. After a moment, Jana began speaking, "The decision not to talk about how I felt during the divorce was made after my one early attempt at trying to describe my feelings backfired completely. I said I'd rather see James dead than married to someone else, and that remark became so completely skewed that gossip reported I wanted him dead. So, after the fiasco it caused, other than my friend Shirley and my counselor, I never shared my feelings with anyone. Why I did just now is a mystery to me. Please accept my apology for subjecting you to my sad ramblings. It's all ancient history; put aside long ago and certainly has no bearing on what happened to James."

"An apology is not necessary," Mike said firmly, adding, "It's hard to separate feelings from facts when you when you have to answer so many personal questions. I'm the one who should apologize for making you relive such unhappy events."

Taken off guard by his statement, it took Jana a moment to respond, saying, "Well, since I've subjected you to part of my sad tale of woe, I'll go ahead and tell you the rest of the story."

When Mike didn't protest, she began, "As I expressed the first time we talked, realizing that James intended claiming Taking It Easy as his alone was a wake-up call to me. I realized I needed to fight to keep what was mine. You need to understand, my entire life had been consumed by James and Taking It Easy, and even though I couldn't stop losing him, there was no way I was going to lose the business. My attorney assured me that, legally, James had no right to exclude me from half of it, warning I just had to be firm and not knuckle under to his shenanigans. And that's exactly what I did."

Mike noted a change in her demeanor as she recalled making that decision. It was obvious that, in spite of the hurt, she'd focused on her goal. Suddenly oblivious to him, Jana continued, "There was a lot of talk among our social circle during the divorce process. I'd been perceived as the perfect wife, always doing whatever James wanted. His buddies always jokingly told him he'd won the lottery when he married me. At first, I was the recipient of all the sympathy; no one could believe James was treating me so callously, dumping me for another woman, but when I began demanding my share of the business, loyalties quickly shifted, and speculation abounded. As rumors flourished about how I was trying to ruin James by taking everything from him, the 'poor Jana' sentiment became the 'poor James' mantra, causing a storm of outrage against me. I was dumbfounded by the reaction of people I'd thought were my friends." Jana picked up her mug and took a sip of coffee, eyeing the man in front of her.

Wordlessly, Mike looked at her, struck by how, in spite of experiencing such devastating heartbreak, she'd managed to pick up the pieces of her broken life and build a new one. Groping for an appropriate response, he remained silent, studying her closely. He didn't want to cause her any further hurt. She'd already suffered more than her share. And her straightforward explanation of the remark she'd made about seeing James dead erased any doubt about Shirley Lewis's statement that Jana had just been trying to describe the deep hurt his betrayal had caused her.

His obsession with proving Jana was responsible for her ex-husband's death was as pointless as chasing rainbows. Nevertheless, in fairness to her, he needed to thoroughly investigate every aspect remotely linking her to it to prove her innocence. The next step was to verify her financial status to completely rule out the possibility she might have needed money badly enough to have him eliminated. Considering how to broach the subject, he surveyed the woman sipping coffee in front of him, his thoughts exploring the best way to begin.

Noticing his expression, Jana set her coffee cup down and looked at him pointedly. "Detective Stone," she said.

Immediately he interrupted her, "If I'm going to call you Jana, you should drop the detective label and call me Mike."

A brief grin spread across her face as she responded, "Okay, Mike, let's get to the nitty-gritty of the reason why you are here today. Let me supply some info that will keep you from struggling to find a tactful way to ask the questions you obviously want to ask."

Again, taken completely off guard by her comment, he threw back his head and laughed. "You are something. I was told you were quite a woman and I'm beginning to understand that comment."

"And I bet I know who told you that," she said immediately. "It was James's best friend, Ray Schuller. He always told James I was far smarter than him. He was one of the few who stood by me."

Mike shook his head at her candor. "Okay, so tell me what you think I want to know," he said, reaching for another slice of the banana bread.

Without hesitating she replied, "You are wondering about my financial status. You want to be sure James' death has nothing to do with my inheriting everything associated with Taking It Easy."

Mike was blown away her statement. It was unusual for someone to present a potential motive for the very crime they were being questioned about. Again, Jana's willingness to offer information did not fit the pattern of a guilty person. Putting all the pieces of evidence together, there was no basis for him to think Jana had been involved in James Browning's murder. She'd have to be the most conniving, evil person he'd ever encountered to do so, and the friendly, attractive woman sitting across from him showed no signs of fitting that description.

Chapter 34

Before he could comment, she continued, "Let me set your mind at ease. I don't need money. I am, was, an only child. My parents were both very successful professionals. My father retired from the military before beginning his career in civil service and my mother was an education consultant for the local college. I was not born until they were both almost 40. Although it sounds like a cliché, my childhood was perfect, filled with happy times and much love. Dad and I were especially close. I will tell you that he was not particularly pleased when I told him I was going to marry James. True to form, he did not spare any words when sharing his opinion of him, saying his observation was that James lacked ambition and was basically lazy, not wanting to work very hard. He told me James would never amount to much. But he also said he wanted me to be happy and that he would accept whatever decision I made."

Mike had remained silent throughout Jana's remarks, studying her intently. Her expression suddenly changed, and with a faraway look in her eye, in a soft tone, she added, "And he did. After that conversation, he never spoke negatively about James again; he walked me down the aisle with a smile on his face. James was my choice and he honored it completely, treating him like a son. James never knew his feelings." At the end of her statement, Jana shook her head and closed her eyes briefly.

Compassion filled Mike as he saw the change that overcame her as she spoke. The realization that her dad had been right about James had surely been very difficult for her to acknowledge. Wanting to reassure her in some way, he cleared his throat, but before he could speak, she continued, "When Dad and Mom died in a plane crash the year after James and I married, our financial status changed dramatically. My inheritance eliminated the need for us to continue working."

She gazed silently into space for a moment and then added,, "James had always talked of owning his own recreational business and, suddenly, we were in a position to allow him to do so. After much discussion, we decided to pursue his dream, purchasing three lots at the new shopping center site bordering the lake. The boat dock and the sporting goods store were built, and we named our business Taking It Easy because the entire enterprise offered recreational items, for those relaxing and enjoying fun things."

Again, she paused, before stating, "The business didn't take all of my inheritance; there was quite a bit left over. The money had been placed in my name in an account separate from the one we established when we married and, ironically, we never bothered to move it to our joint holdings. I really don't know why we didn't; it wasn't a conscious effort on my part to retain the money for myself but in the end, it turned out to be a good decision."

Once again Mike was stuck by Jana's directness. She didn't sound resentful, or hateful. Deciding to dig a little deeper, he asked, "So, Mr. Browning didn't try to get part of the inheritance?"

"No, state law is clear that inheritance is not community property; he knew there was no chance of getting any of it. But I'm fairly certain that was the reason he pursued getting the entire business for himself. He knew I had more than enough money to live on."

Intrigued by the information about the amount of money, Mike found himself wondering just how much Jana had inherited. Although her house was in an elite section of the city, and the furnishings obviously expensive, there was nothing about her to suggest she was rich. She drove a nice SUV, but it wasn't a luxury model, and her clothing looked average to him. Other than a small diamond ring on her right hand, the only jewelry she wore was earrings and they didn't look expensive.

"For the record, I haven't touched a penny of my inheritance since the business was completed. After the divorce, the quarterly payment plus what I earn from my consulting work, which pays very well, is more than adequate for me. Actually, I really don't need to work, but it keeps me busy."

A look of defiance crossed her face as she said, "I insisted on the divorce settlement simply because my parent's money allowed us to build the business and I worked hard to make it successful. James thought I wouldn't fight him because I always did what he wanted, and he knew I had enough money without depending on Taking It Easy. But I was damned if I'd let some young prissy sales rep reap the benefits of my inheritance and my business savvy. So there, once again, you have it in a nutshell," she said, calmly picking up her coffee cup, and watching him closely for his reaction.

At her declaration, Mike he realized he was beginning to really like Jana Arnold. Her open sharing of information during the entire investigation had been impressive. She'd never been hesitant to answer questions or offer explanations in an honest, sincere manner. The hospitality she'd extended had been impressive. Everything he'd heard from her made sense and it almost seemed that she'd been put in an unfair position just because she'd once been married to a man who'd been murdered. His tone congenial, he said, "Well, I guess I don't have to ask any more questions. You've pretty well answered every one I was trying to figure out how to ask."

At his words, Jana let out a sigh, saying, "Although it was hard to do, I've put my life with James behind me. My life changed completely, and I'll admit, sometimes I'm lonely, but I've adjusted. That pretty well sums up the situation." She made her simple, direct statement without a hint of self-pity.

Mike regarded her for a moment before saying, "You are to be commended for the way you've handled the unfortunate happening in your life. I know many people who live in misery because they can't get past things."

"To be perfectly honest, it was the counseling, which was a brutal experience, that made all the difference. But by the time it was over, I understood it was me who'd done all the giving in our relationship. I've spent many, many hours reliving those sessions," Jana said quietly. "Coming to grips with reality took a long time."

That simple statement erased any doubts Mike had about Jana's first interview. It reinforced what he'd suspected all along; her rote delivery of information regarding her life with James Browning was simply a result of the intense counseling she'd undergone. Gathering his briefcase, he rose and started toward the door before suddenly, remembering the last issue needing to be resolved to completely exonerate Jana. Turning, he said, "Oh, there is one thing I forgot to ask," he said.

"What is it?" Jana asked, curious.

"Do you have a gun?"

Chapter 35

This time it was Jana who broke into laughter before answering, "Oh my goodness, what a question to forget! Yes, I have a small handgun." She grinned at him mischievously. "Would you like to see it?"

Mike answered firmly not wanting to joke about his request, "Yes, I need to include information about it in the case report."

Immediately Jana's bantering mood changed. "Well, come on. It's upstairs. I keep it in the nightstand by my bed."

Although it departed from customary protocol, Mike, after a moment's hesitation, decided there was no reason to refuse to go upstairs to examine the gun. He strongly doubted it was in any way related to James's murder, but documentation substantiating that information needed to be included in the report file. So, when Jana pushed her chair back and got up from the table, he did the same and followed her out of the kitchen, down the hallway and up the stairs.

Stepping into the sitting room at the end of the open stairway, Mike noted it was as beautiful as the living room on the first floor. A sofa flanked by end tables with lamps on them sat against one wall facing a large entertainment center featuring a television and stereo along with books, and various decorative items. Two swivel rockers completed the seating options. Magazines on either side of a beautiful arrangement of roses adorned the table in front of the sofa.

"Those roses are exquisite," he commented as he glanced around the room.

"They are from the back yard," Jana said. "The landscapers planted the original bushes the first spring James and I lived here, and we added more every year. We spent hours adding new plants; it was a favorite activity." She paused before adding, "Since the divorce, no additional ones have been planted; I just don't have what it takes. My enthusiasm for continuing the trend has waned, but I make sure the ones that are here are all well cared for. I still love them," Jana offered easily hoping her statement would be another sign she had moved on with her life.

Mike followed her down the hall, but when Jana entered the bedroom, he stopped at the doorway, suddenly conscious that the area was very personal. Watching her make her way to the nightstand beside a king-sized bed, he was struck by the beauty and serene quietness of the surroundings. Light blue walls, bordered by carved molding were a perfect setting for the shimmering white bedspread that boasted an array of huge pillows. Centered in front of a floor-to-ceiling window, a floor lamp's pleated shade hovered over a velvet-covered rocker and matching ottoman that were placed next to a small round table holding several books begging for someone to come read them. An old-fashioned dresser with a mirror and small stool completed the unpretentious, but very tasteful, furnishings. Everything about the room whispered an inviting invitation. His survey was interrupted when Jana motioned for him to come get the object she'd retrieved from the bedside stand. As he walked across the room, she extended a holster holding a gun toward him.

"Here it is," she said, and then added, "Who would have thought I'd ever own a gun?" Shaking her head, she continued, "I was such a mess in the middle of the divorce, scared out of my wits most of the time. When I told my friend Shirley how I felt, she suggested I get a gun. At first I didn't want to, but she said she'd always wanted to take a self-defense course so I decided to do it for her. We took lessons together and, I admit, I did feel better going to bed knowing I had protection in the nightstand."

As Mike took it from her, he noticed how new and unused it looked. He also noted it was a Ruger 38, decidedly different from the Smith and Wesson that had been used to kill James Browning. "When was the last time you shot it?" he asked.

"At the last lesson I had. Frankly, even though it offered some comfort, it was a waste of money to buy the darn thing, and a waste of time going to take lessons. And I've never had a reason to even look at it, much less shoot it. So, I have a gun I have no need for."

Once again Mike was struck by her calm explanation. She spoke without hesitation, offering facts unemotionally, and without excuses. After a moment, he holstered the weapon and handed it back to her. As he watched her put it back in the drawer, he was surprised at the feeling of relief that it wasn't the murder weapon which washed over him.

"Is that all you need?" she asked.

"I think so," he said. "I can finish my report now."

They walked back down the stairs to the front door. Pausing a moment at the front door, he turned and addressed Jana, "Thank you for seeing me again. I hope you understand that these investigations take time."

"I do now," Jana said, adding, "I don't mind talking to you; you make it easy. When I realized interviews with the police would be required, I was both scared and apprehensive. There was no reason to involve me in anything to do with James; my involvement with him ended so long ago. I didn't understand why anyone would want to talk to me. You and Detective Beatty made the whole process easy. You are actually nice, and the best thing is you've listened to all my ranting without thinking I'm a mean, hateful person."

Her comments made Mike regret his relentless pursuit of trying to find a glitch in her testimony that would reveal she'd had something to do with her ex-husband's murder. "Investigations can be tedious," he offered. "That's why people get aggravated with us."

"Don't worry, I'm not put out with you," Jana replied good-naturedly. "I just don't have any worthwhile information to share."

Mike was relieved by her simple response; her lack of offense was reassuring and confirmed she was in no way connected to the murder.

They said goodbye and Mike went to his car. After he drove away, Jana went back into the house, marveling at how, as once again, her dear friend Shirley had unknowingly provided the perfect cover for her. Insisting she needed to buy a gun and take lessons to learn to use it safely had erased any doubt she had firearm expertise.

As Mike drove through the quiet, serene, established older neighborhood, he realized everything about it exuded an atmosphere of dignity and wealth. It crossed his mind how very different it was from the community where James Browning and his new wife lived. James's neighborhood was sparkly and showy, begging for class with an artificial glitter. As his thoughts continued to wander, he recalled how James's new wife was also flashy, new and glittery. It was ironic how the difference in the two neighborhoods was identical to the differences in James's two wives. In no way were they of the same caliber. In his opinion, the sophisticated and genteel Jana Arnold was far above and beyond James's new wife. Jana was quite a lady, and James Browning had been an idiot to let her go.

Chapter 36

For the next few weeks Jana heard nothing from the authorities. Careful to display a proper attitude if someone mentioned James, she withheld all negative comments and opinions about him, displaying a conciliatory attitude. Although curious about the store, she did not contact her attorney regarding its status, instead calling from a phone booth just to see if it was open, and receiving no answer, deducted it was closed. Four weeks after James's death, Jake, her attorney, called and asked her to come in to discuss the status of the business. She hesitated at his request and then said, "You know, I don't see any reason for me to come in, unless you have something I need to sign."

"No, there's nothing requiring your signature right now, but I do have something I need to discuss with you."

Curious, she asked, "What is it?"

"I've been approached by a potential buyer. I've advised them that there has been no discussion about whether or not the business is going to be sold, but it is a significant offer I feel you should consider."

"That's unusual. What is the offer?" she asked, her curiosity piqued.

His answer shocked her. The price offered was three times the amount she and James had paid for the property and at least twice the net worth of the last business statements she'd seen. Wondering about the inconsistency, she asked, "Who made the offer?"

Jake's hesitation made him seem to be reluctant to answer but finally he said, "Ummm, well, it was James' widow. She is very interested in obtaining the business and wants to continue its operation."

For a moment Jana sat motionless as white, hot fury, spread through her. She could barely contain herself. Exhaling, she spoke. Her voice was low and controlled but her words were as bullets on a piercing mission. "That is completely out of the question. You may tell her that it is not an option and that no further discussion will be held regarding it."

"Jana, she offered quite a price. I would advise you not to be hasty in making a decision that you might regret later," Jake ventured cautiously.

"You need to understand one thing and understand it completely," Jana's words were clipped and hard. "The price she's offering is not the issue; I would not sell to her despite any amount she was willing to pay. I don't care what you tell her! Just make up something! Tell her that there is already an offer under consideration or tell her to go to hell! I don't care what you say, as long as you let her know she will never, ever, get the business from me."

There was absolute silence from the other end of the phone. Finally, the attorney cleared his throat and said, "All right, Jana. If that's what you want, I'll deliver your message. I did not intend to upset you, but it is my responsibility to keep you informed of all communication regarding financial possibilities, and that includes anything about Taking It Easy.

"I understand your position," Jana retorted, "and now you understand mine. Please listen very carefully to what I am going to say." Taking a deep breath, she forced herself to be calm. "I will not consider any offer coming from that woman. Further communication from her will be considered harassment and I will address it accordingly through the legal system."

Jake Asher responded in a firm, take-control manner, "You've made yourself perfectly clear, Jana. I will handle all communication from her; your involvement will not be necessary."

"Thank you," Jana and said formally. "I appreciate your understanding my position," and with those words, she ended the conversation.

Replacing the phone receiver, the satisfaction she'd felt from stifling James's wife's offer to buy Taking It Easy suddenly faded. There was no doubt Jake had disapproved of her reaction, thinking it hasty and foolish; he'd cautioned not to reject it without review. In retrospect, the reality that the harshness she'd displayed had not been wise overshadowed any pleasure resulting from refusing the offer. As she analyzed the entire interchange, she was appalled that it might, in fact, raise a red flag. Jake had certainly noticed her animosity; he was a smart man, and little escaped him. She drummed her fingers on the table, considering how she could rectify the situation. Several moments passed as one possibility after another ran through her thoughts. Finally, her mind made up, she reached for the phone, determined to make amends. Jake's secretary took only a minute to connect her to him. His tone was a little curious as he asked, "What's on your mind, Jana?"

Clearing her throat before beginning in a contrite tone, she said, "Jake, I want to apologize for my abruptness about the offer made by James's wife. I don't know why I reacted in such a manner. Maybe it was all the questioning from the detectives, or the realization that the business I once loved so much is gone forever, but it was uncalled for and I'm sorry I was so hateful."

Jake's response confirmed calling him was the right thing to do. "I was surprised you didn't want to find out more about it. You are too good a businessperson to make a decision without examining all the merits of it."

Thinking quickly about how to respond, Jana decided to appeal to Jake's protective side. Making her voice sound weary, she said, "Oh Jake, this whole thing is such a mess! After the divorce was finally over, I made a new life for myself, hoping to put everything behind me. Things were going well until this horrible thing happened, and now I'm back in the midst of chaos again."

Hearing her explanation, she hoped Jake would put aside the uneasiness their earlier conversation aroused. She knew what she told him made sense; the betrayal, suddenly finding herself in the middle of a divorce she'd never dreamed of, had been excruciating.

After all, he'd been right by her side through it all. Surely, for her to react the way she had to James's wife was not unreasonable. Maybe she could fill his mind with the image of the young Jana, who he had watched grow up, the precious daughter of his good friend. Surely, her next plea would tear at his heart.

"Oh, how I wish Dad was here," Jana said longingly, with a hint of a sob in her voice. "He'd know what to do and he'd help me."

Just as she suspected, Jake's response was sure and comforting, "Don't worry Jana. I'm here, and although I'm not your dad, I promise to take care of you."

They ended the conversation with Jake promising to keep in touch. Once again replacing the telephone receiver, Jana let out a sigh of relief, convinced she'd accomplished her goal. Silently promising there would be no more missteps, she vowed to be extra careful in the future.

Chapter 37

The murder investigation continued but nothing new was discovered. The best explanation Mike could offer was that it was an interrupted robbery, that the shooter fled before there was time to get the money from the cash register or take any merchandise. It wasn't really a satisfactory premise, but it seemed to be the only reason for the murder. The file remained open but there wasn't much activity on it.

Interest in the case waned as the weeks wore on. There was some flash flooding due to unexpected rains, and the newspaper and television focused on the damage caused by the storm, abandoning stories about the murder. The file remained on Mike's desk, but since there were no new developments, the investigation stalled. Other issues soon commanded his attention; the James Browning case became a low priority.

Mike was invited to a reception just before Thanksgiving. Usually he avoided those functions, but since there wasn't a ballgame on television, and since the event was hosted by the Youth Foundation which sponsored the Boys Club he worked with, he decided to go. Driving up to the hotel, he silently cursed himself for accepting the invitation. He hated making small talk and he was sure he wouldn't know very many people attending. Sighing, he parked the car and made his way to the entrance, telling himself he wouldn't stay long. After being greeted by the Foundation President and making small talk for a couple of minutes, he made his way to the refreshment table. He was filling his plate when a voice surprised him, "Detective, what a surprise to see you."

Looking up, he saw the person speaking was Jana Arnold. His first thought was that she looked stunning. Her black dress clung to her figure; her blond hair had been pulled back and fastened with a jeweled barrette that let her hair cascade down her back.

Immediately he said, "Well, Ms. Arnold, what did I tell you about calling me 'detective'? I'm Mike."

Laughing, she said, "You got me. And don't you call me Ms. Arnold; I'm Jana; remember?" Her tone was light, and a smile spread across her face as she responded.

He answered, "Okay, Jana, what are you doing here?"

"I volunteer at the kid's drama center, a part of the Youth Foundation which is sponsoring the reception."

"I do recall your involvement with the youth theatre. That must be quite an undertaking. Working with a bunch of kids can be a challenge. I help out with the boys club sponsored by the police department, and while I enjoy it, sometimes those kids can wear me out," he responded.

"I know what you mean. It can be exasperating sometimes, but mostly it's just plain fun working with them," she said.

When they both finished filling their plates, it seemed natural that they would find a table and sit together. Their conversation continued as they enjoyed the food. The host made a brief statement thanking everyone for attending and turned to introduce the small band hired to provide dance music, encouraging everyone to have a good time. Soon the dance floor was filled with couples swaying to the music.

Surprising himself, he asked, "Would you like to dance?"

"Sure, although I warn you it's been a while since I've been on a dance floor," she smiled as she stood.

"The same goes for me, too. I guess we can step on each other's toes," he laughed as he took her arm and lead her to an open spot.

They danced several rounds and returned to the table for coffee. The conversation was light and friendly. He found that he really enjoyed talking to her. He was surprised when people around them began saying their goodbyes and leaving. Looking at his watch, he couldn't believe it was almost 10:00. He hadn't intended to stay over thirty minutes; the time had really flown by.

"My goodness," he exclaimed. "Look at the time. I didn't realize it was this late."

"Do you have an early bedtime?" she asked. "Do you turn into a vampire or something?"

He chuckled in reply. "No but being out like this is unusual for me; I rarely go out anymore."

"Well, you should mend your ways. You might actually enjoy being out," she said.

Almost as if he were thinking out loud, Mike responded, "I've really enjoyed myself tonight. I think it's because I was in such good company." Surprising himself, he asked, "Jana, would you go to dinner with me tomorrow night?"

For a moment, Jana hesitated, trying to think of a way to politely refuse. But then, the thought that she'd really enjoyed her evening with him made her reconsider, and she replied, "Yes, that would be nice."

PART THREE

Chapter 38

And that was how it started. Their first official date took both of them by surprise. In spite of the apprehension each had felt, the evening was relaxing and enjoyable. Jana and Mike were surprised to find how natural their being together was, and how much they enjoyed one another's company. The following weeks found them going to dinner, to the movies, sporting events and spending endless hours just talking. When Jana casually mentioned a play coming to the downtown theatre, and said she'd like to see it, Mike decided to surprise her with tickets. As their friendship blossomed, so did their social life and both were surprised by the pleasure it afforded. One evening, as they pulled into Jana's driveway after having dinner and seeing the latest film release, Jana laughingly said to Mike, "It's so nice to have someone to do things with. And it's really nice not to have to drive myself everywhere."

He retorted, chuckling as he said, "So that's why you go places with me, to keep from driving yourself. I am your chauffeur!"

Her lighthearted reply, "And a good one you are!" left them both in a good mood.

Mike attended the Christmas play Jana and Shirley directed, and she accompanied him to the Boy's Club Christmas party. They spent their time together talking endlessly, sharing stories about their childhood, their travels, and experiences. Mike told Jana about his wife—how she'd been diagnosed with a brain tumor just before their 25th wedding anniversary and died shortly after it. Jana was touched by the sadness that overcame him when he talked about her. It was obvious he'd loved her very much, and still missed her. She didn't talk about her marriage; he understood the betrayal she'd experienced and the journey she'd traveled to move past the hurt and anger. Neither of them thought about their relationship or really considered themselves dating.

For the first time since his wife died, Mike had a bounce in his step; he actually looked forward to weekends and he became interested in the world around him once again. Jana found him charming and she basked in his attentiveness. He was considerate, always wanting to do whatever she chose. It was an easy, non-demanding relationship which both of them enjoyed after the hurt they'd experienced. The week before Christmas, he asked her to have dinner with him on Christmas Eve and was somewhat surprised when she refused his invitation. "Oh," he said, "I guess you have other plans."

She shook her head. "No firm ones, but I do have something I'd like to do."

Disappointed that she didn't want to go out, but trying to understand, he said, "Well, then I think you should do it."

Her smile was mischievous as she replied, "I would really like to have a special celebration, but I'm not sure it's going to happen. It all just depends."

Confused by her remark, Mike queried, "Depends on what?"

"I'm a firm believer Christmas Eve should be celebrated at home. What I would really like is to prepare a special dinner for you, for us to celebrate together. Will you come to my house?" she asked with an expectant look on her face.

Completely surprised by her request, he looked at her for a moment before speaking slowly, "It's been a long time since I had any kind of Christmas celebration; the holiday was very special to my wife and for the most part, I've avoided it since her death."

Hearing his words, disappointment washed over Jana. She started to speak, to tell him she understood, but he interrupted her by saying, "But perhaps it's time to move forward; I accept your invitation."

Somehow knowing his statement was more than just an acceptance to her invitation, she nodded and replied, "Thank you,

Mike. I was hoping you'd agree; but I didn't know how you would feel about celebrating a holiday that held very special memories."

Mike was touched by her sensitivity; her simple acknowledgement confirmed she recognized the holiday had significant meaning for him. The fact she wasn't trying to make him forget his wife and the celebrations they'd shared made it easier for him to accept the invitation.

Later, as she was preparing for bed, Jana considered how Mike had become part of her life. She'd certainly not planned for it to happen; in fact, at first, because of the circumstances that had precipitated their involvement with one another, she'd been reluctant to even be cordial to him.

From the first time she'd met him, his kindness had been both unexpected and comforting; he was always thoughtful and considerate. Immediately, the thought that if he knew the truth about her made her admit it would be a different story. Firmly putting that out of her mind, plans for the upcoming Christmas celebration filled her thoughts. She'd wanted it to be a good evening, but now, somehow, it needed to be utterly fantastic.

Driving home Mike thought about what was happening. Never in his wildest dreams had he imagined being in a relationship with another woman. When his wife died, he'd assumed the rest of his life would be spent alone. His marriage had been happy; he and his wife had loved one another dearly and finding someone to take her place had been unthinkable. He'd steadfastly refused all efforts by his friends to get him involved in dating; he'd had no interest in looking for romance. Pulling into his driveway, he acknowledged that Jana was a delightful person and that the time they spent together was enjoyable, but nothing had changed as far as his interest in pursuing a lasting relationship. He was certain nothing serious was going to come of their friendship, but he did have to admit she was a special person.

Chapter 39

Mike was not sure what to expect when he rang Jana's doorbell Christmas Eve night. Throughout the week, he'd wondered about her wanting to prepare a Christmas supper, finally deciding it was the holiday itself that had prompted her to do so. Part of him was uneasy about the upcoming evening; there had been no hint of what Jana's expectations of it were. Glancing at the bouquet of flowers in his hand, he felt somewhat awkward, wondering just how he'd gotten himself in such a situation. Taking a deep breath, he pressed the doorbell button.

Almost immediately Jana opened the door. She greeted him warmly and exclaimed over the flowers, "They are perfect," she said and took them from him.

Taking his coat and hat and placing them on the rack in the entry hall, she indicated he should follow her into the living room. His gaze took in the beautifully decorated mantle, the exquisite Christmas tree, and the flames dancing brightly in the fireplace. Carols played softly, giving the room a cozy holiday atmosphere. Jana was dressed in black slacks and a red cashmere sweater. Dangly earrings shaped like candy canes completed her festive look.

"Wow," he said. "This is like a scene from a Christmas magazine. You've done a great job."

"I'm glad you like it," she replied with a big smile. "Christmas is my favorite holiday. I'll admit this is the first time I've decorated for it in quite a while, but I really had fun. Our dinner is not quite ready; I thought we'd sit in here while it finishes cooking. I put some appetizers on the coffee table and there's some wassail for us to drink."

They settled in front of the fire, munching on petite quiches and sipping wassail while sharing stories about their childhood

Christmases. It was a comfortable and relaxing atmosphere. When the oven buzzer sounded, Jana went to the kitchen, leaving Mike to contemplate what was taking place. It had been a long time since he'd had any kind of personal Christmas celebration. For the most part, he'd ignored the holiday after his wife died. It was an odd but pleasant feeling to be part of it again.

When Jana summoned him to the dining room, he was surprised by the elegant setting.

The large dining room table had been adjusted to its smallest size, providing an intimate seating arrangement for the two of them. Christmas china accompanied by beautiful sterling flatware, and sparkling crystal goblets, shimmered under the light of the chandelier. The arrangement of holly and roses he'd brought sat between two candlesticks holding lighted tapers. "I didn't expect anything like this," Mike commented as he surveyed the room.

Jana replied quietly, "I haven't served a Christmas meal for the past three years, but I wanted to have one this year. The last few months have brought a renewal of many things for me; I've finally realized life can still be enjoyed. For a while I wasn't sure I would ever find pleasure in anything again."

Surprised by her admission, Mike nodded. "I know what you mean. I feel that way too. It's good to be alive again."

Jana smiled at him and a warm look passed between them. A bit self-conscious, they sat down to eat without further comment. The food was outstanding. When they finished eating, Mike said, "You're quite a cook. That beef tenderloin was out of this world. I never expected such a feast. I'll have to watch my calories for a month."

Jana, obviously pleased by his remarks said, "You don't need to worry about calories tonight; you can splurge for Christmas. Let's have our dessert in front of the fire; you take the coffee carafe to the living room and I'll get the cake."

He filled the mugs on the coffee table before taking his place on the sofa facing the fireplace. When Jana came in the living room, she had two plates piled high with chocolate cake which she placed next to the coffee.

"Oh my goodness, you are a devil!" he exclaimed viewing them. "You know I can't resist chocolate."

She laughed as she slipped off her shoes and sat down beside him, folding her legs under her as she reached for her coffee. They sat for a minute gazing into the fire, not saying anything. The Christmas carols still played softly and there seemed to be no need for words.

"This has been a fantastic evening," he said when he finally spoke. "Thank you for making it so special."

"Thank you for giving me a reason to do something special. As I said before, it's been a long time since I've wanted to put forth the effort," she responded quietly.

"Maybe it's time both of us took charge of our lives again," he suggested. "I'd forgotten how nice doing something like this is."

"Me too," she agreed as she set her mug on the table.

"So, do you think you might want to spend more time with me?" he asked in a teasing tone, not sure how she'd take his comment.

"I think that's a great idea. But I warn you, I'm not a very nice person. You might not like what you discover if you spend more time with me," she warned mischievously.

"I think I'll take the chance. It's worth the gamble," he said as he reached over and took her hand in his.

It was after ten o'clock when Mike left. As Jana washed the dishes and put away the left-over food, she thought what a wonderful evening it had been. She'd refused Mike's offer to help clean the kitchen, saying she could have it all done by the time he got home. It had been a relaxing, enjoyable celebration. For the first time in a long while, she felt like a real person.

Mike's remark about them spending more time together was interesting. Admittedly she enjoyed being with him; he was pleasant and fun to be with. Once again, she wondered how he'd react to learning what she'd done. Knowing his strict adherence to the law, he'd cart her off to jail. There was no reason to pursue that line of thought, she reasoned with herself as she shook her head. All of that was finished.

Chapter 40

The Christmas Eve dinner was a significant milestone for Jana and Mike. Although nothing was said, their being together was different than it had been. When they attended the Police Department's New Year's Eve's party, Mike's friends began questioning whether he was interested in someone for the first time since the death of his wife. He was so well liked, and those close to him had hoped he would find someone to ease the hurt he'd experienced. They'd watched him struggle for so long and had been sad that he was alone. A few knew that Jana was the ex-wife of the man who'd been murdered at the lake, but if anyone was surprised that Mike was dating her, they kept it to themselves. Besides, her easy-going ways, her quick wit and her genuineness made her very likable. And it helped that she seemed to care about Mike and really enjoyed being with him.

Their relationship progressed slowly but steadily over the next few months. James Browning's will was probated and the necessary legal steps were taken to transfer the business and property to Jana. The business had re-opened and was being run by a manager hired by the attorney. Jana was careful not to question the process. She was content to let things progress without intervening. She knew Jake would contact her when her input was needed.

Sure enough, a couple of weeks after the probate was completed, he called, asking, "What do you want to do about the business? Do you want it to remain open with the present manager or do you want it put on the market?"

"It can remain open but put it on the market. I do not want to continue being associated with it. I want to sell it and the property," she informed him.

"There are several entities interested in it," he told her. "We need to decide on a price. I don't think it will take long to sell it."

"That's good to know. Will you get everything appraised and let me know what price we should ask for it? I don't want to be burdened with it any longer than absolutely necessary," she declared firmly.

She discussed the situation with Mike, explaining that the business was part of her life with James and that she did not want to be involved with its operation again. "It would be stepping back in time and I don't have any desire to do that," she told him.

Conversation about the property piqued Mike's interest in the unsolved murder case. He pulled the files and reviewed them again, trying to find any new angle or evidence that might help resolve the murder. After careful review of all the files, nothing that had not already been investigated was uncovered. Once again, the file went on the shelf.

"It is strange that there is nothing to follow-up on," he told Jana as they ate dinner. "It is one of the strangest cases I've ever worked on. It's like someone just shot him for no reason at all."

She looked at him sharply. "What do you think happened?" she asked as she buttered her roll. "Do you still think it was a robbery gone astray?"

"I think that's as good an explanation as any other. Someone must have been spooked off before they could get to the cash register or gather any merchandise. It's unusual, but it does happen," he mused.

"Will the case be closed?" she asked. "Or will it remain open?"

"Technically, it's open, but in actuality, nothing is happening with it. There aren't any witnesses or any kind of leads, so there's nothing we can do. It will just be filed away as a cold case. I hate it when things like this happen," he answered.

"Oh well, that's just the way it is," she said. "Maybe someday it will all be solved."

Mike looked at her. "Does it bother you that it's unsolved?" he asked.

"Not really," she said as she shrugged her shoulders. "I don't think about it. And it really doesn't have anything to do with me. I'd been written off his list long before he was killed, and now he's dead."

Mike nodded. It crossed his mind that her attitude about James's murder was odd, not at all in keeping with her warm, caring nature. But he supposed it was the result of her coping mechanism with the divorce.

Chapter 41

As Jana prepared to go to bed after her evening with Mike, her thoughts turned to their conversation they'd had about James' death. It was odd, but what happened to him never crossed her mind. It was as if the whole episode had been a dream; it was carefully tucked away. "That's exactly where it needs to be," Jana murmured to herself as she crawled into bed. She put the episode out of her mind.

Mike and Jana continued seeing each other, attending events, going to the movies, and eating out. Their relationship was easy; neither of them expected or demanded anything from the other. Mike found being with Jana fun and relaxing. Jana thought Mike was the most caring and dependable person she'd known since her dad.

The anniversary of James Browning's murder passed uneventfully. Jana didn't mention it and neither did Mike. Since technically he was still the lead investigator on the case, it was his responsibility to write a file update but since nothing new had been reported it didn't take long to complete. He didn't mention it to Jana; there was no point.

Life progressed normally; nothing unusual or out of the ordinary happened. Jana stayed busy with her consulting projects; Mike's days were filled with all the duties required of a detective. They spent more and more time together. It was a rare day when they didn't see one another; usually they ate dinner together either at a restaurant or at Jana's house. Their acquaintances began to view them as a couple; seldom were individual invitations extended to either of them.

Jana became the lighthearted person she'd been before her divorce from James, and Mike lost the bewildered look that had identified him since the death of his wife. It was strange, but neither of them thought about what was happening. Carefree, happy, and content, examining the state of their relationship was not a priority.

An innocent, off-the-cuff remark from his partner brought their situation into the forefront of Mike's thoughts. He and Jack were discussing the up-coming cruise Jack and his wife were taking. "I've never been on a cruise," Mike commented, adding, "always thought I'd go on one but just never got around to it."

Jack looked at him for a moment and then said, "Yeah, you really should do that. It would be a perfect honeymoon for you and Jana."

Mike had stared at him blankly. Not knowing how to respond, he'd laughed and remarked about not rushing into anything. Jack's pointed retort, "I hardly think you'd be rushing; it's time for you to do something." His comment was followed by a dissertation about how none of them were getting younger, and that they needed to take advantage of the time they had left, ended the conversation.

For the next couple of weeks, Mike had thought about the exchange between his good friend and himself. Examining his relationship with Jana, he admitted to himself that she had brought both joy and a fulfillment to his life that he'd lost when his wife died. She was in his thoughts daily; he unconsciously planned his day around her. Sure, they kissed and hugged, but their physical relationship had never gone further. From the old school, he didn't pursue more, although he did find her very appealing. Sometimes he didn't want to restrain himself from the feelings he experienced; he was careful to keep within the boundaries he was sure Jana expected, although there were times when he sensed she, too, wanted more.

As he analyzed their situation, the fact that they weren't youngsters, that they had similar life experiences of being married before, that they both had suffered loss, although different kinds, when their marriages ended, and the plain fact that he enjoyed being with her more than anyone, brought him to a startling realization. He wanted her to be a permanent part of his life; not just someone to date but a partner to share all things with; he wanted her to be his wife.

Once he admitted that to himself, he began to formulate a plan in his mind. A bit apprehensively, he went shopping, and then made special plans for the upcoming weekend. Fervently he hoped Jana would approve, but he told himself, if she didn't, he'd have to accept the consequences. As Jack had declared, it was time to do something.

Chapter 42

Jana was surprised when Mike told her where they were going for dinner; it was a very expensive restaurant, not one of their usual casual destinations, but she didn't comment. They ate, laughing and talking and enjoying each other's company as always. It wasn't until they had finished eating and the waiter appeared with a bottle of champagne and glasses that she became curious.

"What's all this?" she asked, a puzzled look on her face. "Is there something going on I don't know about?"

"Well, I guess you could say that," Mike replied. I have a surprise for you, and I hope you will be pleased," he said nervously.

"A surprise? What is it?" she probed.

Casually he reached in his coat pocket and withdrew a velvet box. "Jana, I think you know I care about you. In fact, saying I care is not exactly the truth; I've fallen in love with you and I'd like for you to be my wife. Will you marry me?" he asked as he opened the box to reveal a beautiful emerald cut diamond ring.

For a moment Jana sat completely still. Then with tears in her eyes, she looked at him. "Oh Mike, I can't believe this. You are the dearest person in the world. And I love you, too."

"So, you will marry me?" he asked.

"I would love to marry you. You make me so happy," she answered softly. "You just don't know what kind of girl you're getting. If you did, you'd run."

He chuckled. "I know enough about you to want you to be my wife. You are making me the happiest man alive," he said as he leaned over and kissed her. He took her hand and slid the ring on her finger before picking up the champagne flute, clicking his glass against hers. The rest of the evening was spent making plans, discussing what kind of wedding would be appropriate, where they would live and a thousand other details their decision to marry had brought to the surface. His goodnight kiss sealed their commitment.

Driving home, Mike's heart overflowed with happiness; after losing his wife he'd thought his life would always be meaningless. The darkness that had surrounded him was now lifted, replaced by joy and anticipation of a new beginning. Jana had changed everything for him. She was such a good person; she made him very happy.

Heading up the stairs, Jana, too, was filled with happiness. Gazing at the beautiful ring on her finger, she was overcome with love for Mike. But a dark element that wouldn't go away hovered in the back of her mind and her thoughts turned to James and his untimely end. Part of her wanted to confess to Mike what she'd done but knowing the result of such a confession halted any decision to do so. It was ironic that his death had been the reason she'd met Mike. "That's the best thing you ever did for me, James Browning," she said, as she slid into bed.

Chapter 43

The next morning Jana called Shirley and invited her to lunch. As soon as they sat down, she told Shirley her news, and her friend was ecstatic. "Oh Jana, I've prayed for you to find someone to share your life with," she said as she hugged her. "And Mike is the best person in the world; he's so good and caring. He is one in a million."

For a moment, Shirley's exuberant comments about Mike hit Jana like a ton of bricks. The cold hard fact that she wasn't a good person; that she was, in fact, a murderer, washed over her. An overwhelming desire to confess her crime to Shirley overtook the happiness of the occasion. Unaware of Jana's dilemma, Shirley's chatter and enthusiasm over the news of the upcoming wedding interrupted Jana's thoughts, causing her to put them aside.

She and Shirley were deeply engrossed in wedding plans when Jana's phone rang. "It's Jake, my attorney," Jana said looking at the caller ID.

"Go ahead and take it," Shirley replied.

Jana answered and right away, the attorney told her there had been several offers to buy the business. When she asked for the details, he gave her the numbers and then, hesitantly, told her he wanted to talk to her about something.

"What is it?" she asked. He never asked her permission to discuss anything.

"I know you told me you would not consider any offer Mrs. Browning made, but I feel obligated to inform you she has put another one on the table and it is more than generous. In fact, it is far above the price we would ask for the property. I think you should at least review her proposal."

Jana did not hesitate to answer, and her irritation was unmistakable, "Jake, I am not interested in her offer. I thought I made that perfectly clear previously."

"But Jana," he countered, "Money is money. Won't you at least consider it?" he said.

"No, I will not. You need to understand the money she is offering is money that is rightfully mine in the first place; money that she inherited when James died. I paid those insurance premiums for years before she came along. I will not sell to her. I will not allow her to have a business I put my heart and soul into for years," her voice was shaking as she replied.

"All right; the matter is settled," he conceded. "I will tell her the offer is refused."

"Thank you. I'm glad you understand." Jana's words, clipped and cold, ended the discussion. Their conversation continued for a few minutes more, and when it ended, Jana sat down across from Shirley and rubbed her forehead.

"I can't make him understand that I won't sell Taking It Easy to James' wife," she said wearily. "She keeps calling with offers, in spite of all the rejections she's received. Jake thinks I'm being dumb not to consider selling to her. He just doesn't understand how she tore my whole world apart. I guess I'm going to have to go see her and explain it's useless for her to keep calling. I'm sick of her and I want to make sure she understands."

Shirley was surprised at the change in Jana's demeanor. Very angry, she'd suddenly become an entirely different person from the happy, carefree bride-to-be she'd been before the phone call. Obviously, her attitude toward James's widow had not changed. It was frightening to think she might be reverting back to the same frame of mind she'd been in during the divorce process. Shirley was afraid that Jana was about to become mired in a debate that would only bring her more heartache.

Carefully she observed her friend whose entire body was tense and rigid, with narrowed eyes and tightly clenched hands. At once Shirley was reminded of the turmoil that had engulfed Jana during the divorce. Quietly, but firmly, she addressed her friend, "Jana, don't let her into your life. She isn't worth it. You've made your position very clear to your attorney; now let it go and let him handle it. A confrontation with you is exactly what she wants. She knows you won't sell to her, but she's going to keep pestering you. She enjoys upsetting you. Let it go. That way you win, not her."

As Shirley's words sank into Jana's mind, she smiled. "Shirley, there you go again, bringing complete sense to what I should do. You are right. That's what she wants. It's your good sense that keeps me in line; I can't figure anything out for myself. I don't know what I'd do without you."

The two women hugged, and the subject of selling to Mrs. Browning was put to rest. Later that night, Jana thought about Shirley's comments. She had no idea why the woman kept pestering her, but Shirley was absolutely right. Ignoring her was far better than getting into a confrontation. Once again Shirley had protected her. Climbing into bed, she was thankful for such a good friend.

Chapter 44

Mike was at his desk when the receptionist approached him, a puzzled look on her face.

"There's a woman out front requesting to speak to someone about the James Browning murder investigation. She is adamant that she has information about the case."

Immediately, Mike stood up. "Bring her into the conference room," he instructed. He picked up his tape recorder and a legal pad and made his way to the large room at the end of the hall. His partner, Jack, had not yet arrived for his shift, but Mike was confident he could handle the situation alone.

He watched as the receptionist escorted a woman down the hall. He thought he'd seen her before but couldn't remember who she was. She was attractive in a flashy sort of way. Her red hair was obviously dyed; she wore heavy make-up and her jewelry was gaudy. Mentally he compared her to Jana, who would never dress or look the way this woman did.

She held out her hand, saying, "Detective Stone, thank you for meeting with me. I have some information about James Browning's murder."

It was then that he remembered her. She was Browning's wife...widow. He had met her; the first time was the day Browning had died. Then he and his partner had interviewed her the following day.

After pulling out a chair for her and motioning for her to be seated, and then sitting down across from her, he said, "We've met before."

"Have we?" she asked. "I don't remember."

"It was the day Mr. Browning died and then the day after. My partner and I came to your house."

"Oh, of course. I'm sorry. I forgot. But I was so upset then. I don't remember much about those days at all."

"That's understandable, Mrs. Browning. What information brings you here today?" he said, smoothing over her forgetfulness.

"I know who killed James," she stated matter-of-factly.

"When did you find out who did it?" he asked.

"Well, I've always suspected her, but recently I've put everything together."

Mike looked at the woman sitting before him. "Who do you think it was?" he asked.

"I don't think; I know! It was Jana Arnold, James's ex-wife," she said with assurance.

Mike looked at the woman in total disbelief. His long years of training allowed him to remain non-committal; his expression betrayed none of the shock he felt. His mind racing, he wondered, *how on earth she could think Jana killed James Browning? Why would she be saying something like that?*

Immediately, he realized he couldn't conduct the interview without another person present. Calmly, he addressed Mrs. Browning, "Excuse me a moment, please. I think my partner would like to be included in our meeting."

Walking away from the conference table, he prayed Jack would be at his desk, available to join him for the interview. As he rounded the corner, he was relieved to see Jack walking toward him. Quickly, he explained the situation and both men returned to the conference room. Mike re-introduced Mrs. Browning to Jack, and after they were both seated, he cleared his throat. After recording a few statements including the date, time and who was present in the meeting, he pushed the tape recorder to the side and took out the legal pad. Then he said, "For the record, let's start at the beginning. Tell me everything you know that led you to the conclusion about your husband's murderer. First of all, could you tell me why you think Jana Arnold did it?"

"Well, I don't know if you found this out but everyone who knows her is well aware of how angry she was when James divorced her. She fought with everything possible to get all of his money and the business and property. She was relentless in her pursuit to ruin him financially. You can ask anyone who knew them and they'll tell you how hateful she was," she replied in a know-it-all tone Mike had heard many times before from people who were so sure of what they were saying.

"That may be true," Mike said calmly, "but that doesn't mean she killed him."

"Well, she did! You need to understand that she couldn't stand losing him to me. In addition, she couldn't stand losing the business. It took forever for the divorce agreement to be finalized; her demands were outlandish but there was no changing them. Her hot-shot lawyer made it perfectly clear that no compromises would be considered. There was no way James was going to be able to fight her. You can ask any of their friends about how angry and vindictive she was through the whole process."

Mike nodded as the woman spoke. Her statements basically confirmed what Jana had had told him during the initial interview he and Jack had with her. But those facts didn't make her a murderer.

Pausing for a moment, the woman looked at him to see his reaction, and then continued in a smug manner. "You probably don't know that she bought a gun and took lessons learning how to use it. She told people she'd rather see James dead than married to me. She made a plan and when she thought everyone had forgotten the things she'd said, she went to the store and killed him. That's why no money was taken; it wasn't a robbery—it was just her getting even with James and with me."

She'd spoken with such conviction that Mike was taken aback. "It's been a long time since the crime, and you haven't said anything before now. When did you make that decision? Do you have any proof, or evidence that she is guilty?" Mike asked, holding his breath as he waited for her reply.

Chapter 45

"It's really very simple. She knew he spent most of his time outside where the boats and paddle boards were. She went into the store, just waited until James was alone, then she shot him."

Mike gazed at the woman, wondering why she hadn't come forward sooner if she felt so strongly about Jana's guilt. "What made you wait so long to come voice your opinion?" his voice was curious as he asked the question.

Once again, the woman spoke assuredly. "Well you see, I've offered to buy the business and property from her. There was some sort of stupid stipulation that she would inherit it if anything happened to James. I did not know about it until after his death; I can tell you it would never have been in place had I known, but when I found out, I made an offer to buy it because it meant so much to James."

"I see," Mike interjected intending to ask her to explain what the stipulation had to do with the murder but before he spoke, she began talking.

"Her attorney told me that she declined my offer. He said she was not interested; he didn't state a counter amount or anything and the property is still on the market at the much lower price than the offer I made."

"So, refusing your offer means she killed James?" Mike asked. "You don't have any other evidence to show she's guilty?"

"No, I don't need any. My offer was three times what the business is worth. She turned it down because she doesn't want me to have the business any more than she wanted me to have James. And it was a way for her to re-claim the things they worked on together."

Mike made himself speak slowly and in a thoughtful manner. "I understand your frustration, Mrs. Browning. I also understand that you might think Ms. Arnold killed your husband. But there is no evidence that she is any way connected with his murder. The investigation has been thorough: no weapon was found; no DNA was present; nothing was there to identify the person who did this. The best explanation is that it was an interrupted robbery. I'm sorry but the fact that your offer to buy the business was refused does not mean a crime was committed."

She looked at him, unwilling to accept what he was saying. In a cold, uncompromising voice she said, "You don't understand. I know she killed him."

He met her gaze, and spoke in a firm, no-nonsense voice, "Mrs. Browning, I understand your frustration, but there is no evidence that Ms. Arnold is the person who killed your husband. Unfortunately, nothing conclusive has been discovered; the case is still open, and the department continues to follow through on any information received."

A scathing look accompanied her reply, "Did you investigate her? Do you know where she was at the time he was killed?"

"Yes, Ms. Arnold was thoroughly investigated. Hours were spent reviewing all feasible possibilities, but nothing was found to link her to his death. Unless you can furnish something that was overlooked which points to her, or to anyone else for that matter, the investigation is currently at a standstill. I'm sorry."

For a long moment, she sat silently. And then, her obvious disgust reflected in her tone, she replied, "I see. She's fooled all of you. It's obvious you think because she is such a nice society lady, she would never do anything so brutal."

Impatient with her lack of confidence in the department and especially his investigative capabilities, Mike leveled his gaze to meet her eyes and spoke firmly, "I don't care if she is a nice society lady as you put it, or a despicable tramp; my job is to solve crimes regardless of who commits them. There is simply no proof that Ms. Arnold committed that crime."

Abruptly, she stood and shouldered her handbag. Her voice rising angrily, she declared, "I know what I know. I can't prove it yet, but she is guilty. Her refusal to sell me the business confirmed what I thought all along. She may have you fooled, but she can't fool me." And with that comment, she tossed her head and left the room. Mike walked out with her, hearing the sound of her high heels echoing as she made her exit.

Mike returned to the room where Jack still sat. Shaking his head, he said, "Makes no sense to me. It isn't unusual for someone to be frustrated with an investigation, but I've never seen anyone with an attitude like the one we just encountered. But, Mike, you need to be careful. Mrs. Browning could cause a lot of trouble if she realized you and Jana are going to be married. Given your relationship with Jana, we must make sure we document the entire visit precisely so no one can question our integrity on this case. Maybe we should review it immediately with the Chief."

"I thought about that. That's why I wanted you in the interview. Will you sign off on the report?"

"Sure, that's no problem," Jack said "and, I'll take the lead when we talk to the Chief."

Once back at his desk, Mike very carefully wrote his report about the meeting with Mrs. Browning. He included her comments about the department's investigation, as well as her venomous explanation as to why Jana Arnold had committed the murder. He offered no opinion, just stated the facts.

Chapter 46

Later, when Mike met Jana at the little Italian restaurant near her house, he told her about the visit he'd had from James's widow. Jana listened as he recounted the conversation accusing her of killing James. Anger washed over her as she heard the things that had been said. It was ironic that stupid woman could have any inkling of the way she felt. Heart racing, she made herself appear amused, and somewhat aggravated as she said, "Well, it sounds like she got the message that I would never sell to her. And I guess she knows she'll never be my best friend." Mike smiled at her remarks; that was Jana.

Nonchalantly she wound spaghetti around her fork before asking, in an off-hand manner, "What exactly is the status of the investigation? Will her visit cause it to be reopened?"

Mike took a swallow of his iced tea before he replied. "No, she didn't offer anything to follow up on. She appeared vindictive and determined to get me to agree that your refusal to sell to her made you James's killer. I think she understood her visit was futile. Jack and I completed our report and filed the tape recording along with it. It will become part of the file, but other than that, nothing else will happen."

"Was I ever considered a suspect, Mike?" Jana asked with curiosity in her voice. "I never thought I was other than the visits from you and Jack; no one else contacted me. It's disturbing that all that could start again with the accusation from that woman."

"Don't worry about it, Jana. There is no reason for anyone to suspect you. A thorough investigation was done documenting your whereabouts at the time of the murder. Every aspect of your alibi was thoroughly researched. There was no indication whatsoever you were involved in James Browning's murder," Mike said as he reached over and put his arm around her shoulder.

"It worries me Mike," Jana said. "If that woman had met with anyone but you, there's no telling what would have happened. She's angry because I didn't accept her offer to buy Taking It Easy and is using it to get back at me. The simple truth is I've been over the fact that she was married to James for a long time, but I don't want her to continue benefitting from the business I put so much effort into. She needs to look somewhere else for her money."

The detective part of Mike noted that Jana's statement was firm, but not laced with any hostility or vindictiveness. Understanding she was upset over the accusation and wanting to assure her she had nothing to worry about, he said, "Well I wanted to tell you she'd been to the station and that I'd been the lucky one to conduct the interview. Her accusation will be nothing more than a sentence in the case file. You can quit worrying."

They finished their dinner, talking of other things and made their way to the movie theatre. The evening was pleasant and when Mike kissed Jana good night, there was an air of contentment. As Jana puttered about the kitchen, she thought about her conversation with Mike. Recalling Shirley's advice about ignoring James's wife, she smiled. That had been wise counsel; it had prevented any confrontation between the two of them that might have resulted in revealing something better left hidden. There was no reason to be concerned about anything having to do with James or his stupid wife. All she needed to do was keep quiet and go about her business as usual. Her secret was hers alone; it would never be shared with anyone. It did cross her mind that it really was a shame his wife hadn't been in the store with him when he died; both of them could have been eliminated. For a moment she was shocked by her thought, but then she brushed it aside. There was no reason to drudge up any of that old business. She had better things to think about. There was a wedding on her horizon!

Chapter 47

As they made preparations for their future, Jana had a concern she wasn't sure Mike would share. Not knowing how he would feel about it, she was hesitant to broach the subject, but it weighed on her mind. After considerable thought, she decided to talk to him about it. As they were eating dinner, timidly she said, "Mike I want to ask you something but I'm a little afraid about how you will react."

Mike responded quickly, "Unless you are going to tell me you've changed your mind about becoming my wife, just tell me. I'm sure I can handle whatever it is."

Clearing her throat before she spoke, she said, "How do you feel about us getting a different house, selling this one and moving into a new place?"

"That would be fine with me Jana just as long as we're moving together. I didn't think you'd want to give up this place. It is beautiful, and you've put so much effort into making it special."

Jana looked at him appreciatively before replying, "It has been my home for many years. My parents gave it to me, and it was the place I began my life with James; it was special to me. When we divorced, I worked hard to make it something different, and, with Shirley's help, I was able to do that. But it is part of a time that is over for me. I want to create something for us that doesn't have any connections with the past. Beginning our life together in new surroundings would make sure that what we have is ours and ours alone."

Mike sat quietly for a moment and Jana couldn't read his thoughts. Afraid he didn't want to undertake finding another house, she offered, "If you don't feel the same way, we can stay here."

When Mike finally responded, he said, "Jana, what you just told me about wanting to create something special for the two of us means more to me than I can say. I would be delighted for us to find a place that's just our own, a place where we can make our own memories without any history attached to them."

His words filled Jana's heart; once again she was overcome by the pure goodness of the man who was soon to be her husband.

"Let's look around and see what we can find. Put this place on the market; I'm sure it will sell quickly," Mike said.

And sure enough, within the month they'd found a new house, and a contract was pending on the place that had been her home for almost two decades. She plunged into decorating their new home, not hesitating to discard much of her furniture, wanting to start completely over with Mike. She did keep her piano and her mother's desk, along with the trunk holding her father's special papers and pictures. The draw string bag that had held her Dad's revolver was carefully folded and placed on top of them, although there was nothing to suggest what its original purpose had been.

When the new house was in order, Jana was filled with a peacefulness that had eluded her for a long time. Her life was finally in order. There was nothing left to remind her of James Browning. There was no reason to spend any time or energy dwelling on the past. What was done was done. She had no regrets.

Chapter 48

They chose the Sunday afternoon before Thanksgiving as their wedding date. Jana and Shirley worked together planning both the wedding and reception. Fifty invitations were mailed and fifty RSVP's confirming attendance verified how delighted their friends were about their marriage. Everything about the preparation was surreal to Jana; she'd never imagined getting married again.

Jana shopped and shopped for just the right dress before finally finding a pale blue sheath she thought was appropriate. She decided not to wear anything in her hair except a jeweled clip to hold it in place. She woke on the day of her wedding full of anticipation and happiness. Briefly her mind went back to the day of her first wedding, but quickly all thoughts of it were cast aside. The long practice of squelching any thought of James, their life together, and what had happened to him, had faded those recollections, and recalling them had no point. There was no reason to remember any of it, especially the final episode they'd shared together. She was well aware it was a secret never to be shared with anyone. Drinking her coffee and anticipating the joyous day before her, once again, she acknowledged the importance of leaving that deed buried forever. Well aware it had to be kept secret, with renewed resolution she rose from the table and went to get ready for her wedding.

In a charming little chapel not far from the police station, at four o'clock in the afternoon, Mike and Jana walked down the aisle together to become husband and wife. It was a touching ceremony with both of them promising the rest of their lives to each other.

The reception was held in the ballroom of one of the larger downtown hotels. Thanks to Shirley, who had orchestrated the entire event, beautifully decorated tables, excellent food, and a stunning wedding cake highlighted the festivities. Everyone enjoyed the celebration; their friends were delighted to see the two of them so happy. When the reception was over, Shirley helped Jana change from her wedding dress into traveling clothes. As she carefully folded the dress Jana had worn and placed it in a storage bag, thoughts of Jana's wedding to James invaded her thoughts. It was ironic that she was witnessing the beginning of her dear friend's second marriage, but her heart was filled with joy. Jana deserved to be happy after all she'd been through and she was confident Mike was the key to making it happen. He wasn't anything at all like James.

As the happy newlyweds departed for the airport to begin their honeymoon trip, the guests clapped and laughed. Everyone was so pleased for them. Mike had planned their trip, without consulting Jana who'd been content to be surprised with whatever agenda he selected. Their destination was a quiet resort on the Virginia Beach coast. The large room featured a whirlpool spa and a balcony with a magnificent view of the beautiful ocean. The restaurant was outstanding. Quaint trolleys supplied transportation to the community theatre and the many unique shops in the adjoining town. Jana felt like a princess; Mike devoted himself to making sure every day was filled with a new adventure. It was the perfect beginning for the rest of their life together.

As they began their married life, Jana was happier than she'd ever imagined being. Mike continued treating her like a princess, spoiling her in every way possible. He delighted in surprising her: little gifts, special outings to the theatre, and unexpected trips filled every day with joy. Jana was so happy.

On the very rare occasions when memories of James invaded her thoughts, she quickly pushed them aside. Her life with Mike had erased all the bitterness and anger associated with him and their failed marriage.

Chapter 49

But sometimes, when least expected, routine events offer disturbing surprises and Jana was faced with one threatening incident right before their first wedding anniversary. The local Police Association's annual picnic, an event Mike really enjoyed, was scheduled and he'd wanted her to go with him. It was a huge event, showcasing the various departments and featuring demonstrations of training exercises required by incoming cadets. Attendees were invited to try their hand at the various stations. Mike was interested in the weapons training demo; a firing range had been set up and he'd told Jana he wanted to see it. As they approached the cordoned off area, Jana couldn't believe her eyes. It had been over twenty years but standing before her was the owner of the firing range she and her dad had gone to for her to learn to handle a firearm. He didn't look the same; his hair had turned gray and was receding above his forehead. His face was lined, and his posture no longer ramrod straight, as it had been when she'd spent so much time at the firing range. But it was him, there was no doubt.

Momentarily, panic seized her. All she could think about was that Mike was about to discover her lie about her experience using guns. Frantically, she tried to formulate an explanation for her omission. Deliberately forcing herself to calm down, and organize her jumbled thoughts, she took a deep breath. Slowly common sense overtook the panic as she acknowledged silently, that if he looked different, she did too; the changes the years had brought had altered her appearance as much as they had altered his. Plus, the large sunhat and dark glasses hid her features. And they were far away from the place the interactions had taken place.

Suddenly, they were standing before the man. When Mike introduced himself and Jana, she didn't speak. The man didn't pay much attention to her; he and Mike discussed the training program. After a few minutes, the man asked if they'd like to try their hand at shooting. Mike declined and Jana shook her head. When the man turned his full attention to Jana, he remarked thoughtfully, "You remind me of someone; you look familiar."

Mike laughed at his remark and said teasingly, "Oh, so you know another beautiful woman?"

The man grinned, replying, "I've taught many pretty women to shoot. And if I do say so myself, I've always done a good job."

"Well I can guarantee you my wife wasn't one of your students. She did take some lessons at a local sporting goods store and even bought a gun a few years ago, but she hasn't even touched it since."

Jana smiled disarmingly, and said in a low voice, "My husband has a low opinion of my abilities with a gun."

They chatted for a few minutes longer before moving away from the firing range. Jana noticed how the instructor kept staring at her as she and Mike walked away. Purposely she steered Mike away from him and his inquiring gaze. Jana was unnerved by the encounter, even though the man had not recognized her. Her hands shook, and her heart raced as she considered what could have ensued if he had.

Chapter 50

Try as she might, Jana could not put the afternoon encounter out of her mind. Always before, when something reminded her of James, she'd been able to subdue it, but today had been different. The reality that if the owner of the firing range had recognized her and commented about her expertise with weapons it would have been disastrous made her realize how precarious her situation really was. If, for whatever reason some isolated incident caused questions about her behavior, it was possible her actions might raise suspicions. She'd never been uneasy before, but while her alibi was perfect there might be mitigating circumstances that would cause further investigation and uncover some flaw. It was not a good proposition.

That evening, when she and Mike were sitting on the patio beside the pool, Jana made the decision to confess her secret to Mike. Knowing it would probably destroy their life together, but not wanting to continue hiding anything from him, hesitantly, she began, "Mike, there are things about me you don't know. It's time for me to tell you."

Mike looked at her quizzically. The detective in him was suddenly alerted as he noted the expression on her face, the apprehension in her voice, and her overall uncertainty. He took a sip of his iced tea, and waited without saying anything, for her to continue.

"I'm not the person you think I am," she said haltingly as she bowed her head. "There are things in my life that would shock you; things you would never approve of. You should have been told before we married, but the time never seemed right and foolishly, my decision was to ignore them. But it's time to tell you."

Mike couldn't imagine what was bothering her. Kind, sweet, Jana, who always went out of her way to help others, had something weighing heavily on her mind. Observing her, he thought about all she'd been through, how she'd been betrayed, how a whole life had been buried and how she'd started over, learning to put aside her hurt. Seeing the tears in her eyes as she looked so helplessly at him, and watching her swallow as she prepared to speak, Mike's heart was filled with love for the precious woman in front of him. Before she could continue, he spoke, "Jana, I don't have any idea what's bothering you, but before you go off on some tangent, please listen to me."

For a fleeting moment, Jana wondered if he knew what she was going to confess, but then, just as quickly, she dismissed the idea. Her Mike, the man so dedicated to law and truth, would never have let something so wrong go unpunished. Expectantly, she waited for his words.

Mike spoke quietly, his tone patient and deliberate, saying, "Jana, we were not youngsters when we met; we came from different backgrounds and our lives had presented us with varied experiences. We'd both been married, and although our marriages were not anything alike, the role of husband and wife was not unfamiliar to either of us. We moved forward with our commitment to one another, putting the past behind us."

Mike paused and looked at Jana. When she didn't comment, he began speaking again.

"The truth of it is that in the course of living life, people make unwise decisions and mistakes. No one is perfect. I did things I'm not proud of; some of my escapades were just plain stupid, and I suspect you made decisions or did things you came to regret. When we met and fell in love and decided to spend the rest of our lives together, it was a new beginning—a time to let things from the past remain there. I see no point in either of us dredging up some mistake that was made before we even knew one another. Whatever happened in our past has no bearing on the love we have for each other. I'd rather we enjoy our life and be thankful, knowing we are blessed to have each other. I don't need or want to know about something you did before we met. You can't change whatever it was, and our happiness has not been disturbed because of it. Dredging up some long-ago deed won't accomplish anything; whatever is bothering you, in my opinion, is something that's better left alone. I hope you feel the same way about me; I don't want to confess every evil thing I've done." He paused for a moment and then said lightly, "You might not be able to forgive me and then what would I do? Our life together would end but it wouldn't change my mistake. Both of us would have to face the future alone, unhappy and deprived of the fulfilling life we have with one another."

For a moment, Jana wanted to contradict him; to argue that he didn't understand the magnitude of her deed. But the wisdom of his words struck through her, and she stopped. The simple fact was that what he said was true. There was no changing what had been done. Confessing it wouldn't accomplish anything good; it would only destroy the life they had together. Although she knew her deed was far more than some insignificant mistake, what he was saying did make sense. Nothing would be gained from admitting she was responsible for James's death; in fact, the admission would destroy everything good that had happened after it occurred. Wordlessly, she rose from her chair and went to him. He pulled her onto his lap and said, "Can you put whatever is bothering you to rest? Isn't knowing I love you enough? I just want to be sure you love me."

"I do love you, Mike. More than you can imagine. I'll never ever stop loving you," she whispered as she wrapped her arms around him, once again vowing to keep her secret.

Chapter 51

The following day Jana spent more time thinking about James and what she'd done. Truthfully, she wasn't sorry. There had been no remorse on her part; eliminating him had been the only option she'd had to avoid the pain his presence caused her. As far as she knew, he wasn't missed by anyone except the sleazy slut he'd married, and she didn't count. Mike's words made more sense than her wild desire to clear her conscious. She was thankful Mike had reinforced her decision to leave the past behind.

Other than the quarterly payments Jana received, Taking It Easy was not part of their life. All issues concerning it were handled by Jana's attorney. Her explanation that it belonged, just as did everything connected to James, in the past and no longer mattered, was completely acceptable to Mike. When Jake Asher contacted her, advising a 3.5-million-dollar offer had been made to buy it, she told Mike she wanted to sell. Jana had never visited the store after James's death. Telling Jake she had no desire to know them, she'd declined to meet the new owners and also declined their generous offer for her to go choose whatever she wanted from the store. The entire transaction was handled by her attorney.

The money from the sale had a significant impact on Mike and Jana's life. Mike resigned from the police force; Jana ended her consulting career. They traveled, entertained friends, and reveled in their companionship. The life they lived did not include conversations about the past. It was not necessary to recall old events.

One Sunday morning shortly after celebrating their 5th wedding anniversary, Jana opened the newspaper to see a startling headline. Her heart skipped a beat as she read "Cold cases to be reopened by the local police department."

Following the headline was a lengthy article outlining three cold cases: the murder of a homeless woman that had occurred three years before, a hit and run death from the year before and the murder of a well-known businessman, James Browning that happened almost eight years before. Quickly she scanned the article. To her relief the writer confirmed that no new evidence had been discovered in any of the cases. James's murder was described as being the most puzzling of the three incidents. She read slowly, critically absorbing the information presented. She wanted to be sure she was aware of everything the article included.

When Mike came in the kitchen, she held the paper out to him. "Look at this," she said. "I thought all that was buried and dead. Why do you think it's being brought up again?"

Mike took the paper and scanned the article. "It's not unusual for cold cases to be reviewed," he replied. "No police department likes not having resolution to crimes committed. Probably some new detective was bored and had nothing to do and began digging in the old files."

"How will they go about it," she asked as she buttered some toast for him.

"Review of all the files, interviews with all the interested parties to see if their stories are the same and a look at any evidence that was collected at the time of the incident. Most likely, you will be contacted."

"Oh my goodness!" She exclaimed, "I don't want to be bothered with all that again. Can't I just refuse to meet with them?"

He chuckled as he answered, "Well if you want to sound an alarm on their radar, go ahead and refuse. That would be a sure way to pique their interest in you as a suspect. You might as well get prepared to go over everything again."

She sighed as he folded the newspaper and laid it on the buffet behind him. "Oh well, I guess I have no choice in the matter. I hope they make their visit short and sweet."

"Well, one thing's for sure," he said as he reached for her hand. "You won't be meeting a future husband at the interview like you did at the last one. At least you better not be. That was one of the most productive interviews I've ever conducted even if I didn't learn anything about the crime I was investigating."

"Oh you," she said as she planted a kiss on his cheek.

The rest of the morning passed as usual. They finished breakfast, read the paper, went for a walk in the park. The day passed uneventfully. Jana didn't allow herself to think about the reopening of the murder case. She told herself she'd think about it later.

Chapter 52

A couple of weeks passed before Jana was contacted concerning the cold case. The caller introduced himself as Detective Wayne Bradley. He carefully explained he was with the police department and said that he would like to meet with her regarding the unsolved case involving her ex-husband.

"I'm happy to meet with you, but it will be a waste of your time," she said, forcing herself to be pleasant. He ignored her comment and asked if she would rather come to the police station or meet somewhere else. Jana suggested he come to her house and arrangements were set for the interview. Hanging up the phone, she sighed and shook her head.

When she told Mike about the upcoming meeting, he told her he would be there, too. When she protested, he informed her she didn't have a choice. "If my wife is being questioned, I'm going to be by her side," he said.

Wayne Bradley was young, far younger than Mike had been when he'd investigated the murder. It was obvious that he didn't have the expertise of an experienced investigator, but what he lacked in that department, he made up for with enthusiasm.

He started by asking her to recount her actions the day of the murder. Jana didn't want it to appear that her story had been rehearsed, nor did she want to be too vague. She looked at Mike for reassurance as she recounted that she'd shopped and prepared for a party. The detective kept referring to a folder filled with notes and Jana got the impression he wasn't adept at interviewing. Rather than offer much information she waited for him to ask specific questions. He asked what she did after her shopping trip, and she recounted that she'd prepared for a party that was being held at her house. She mentioned Shirley and he immediately told her that he would be questioning her as well. Jana began to relax when she realized he didn't have any new information, nor did he appear to know exactly what direction the new investigation should take.

When he'd established her alibi, she thought he would end the interview. Instead, he crossed his arms, leaned back, and asked, "How did you feel about your ex-husband, Mrs. Stone?"

Jana was startled by the question. She hadn't expected to discuss anything except her actions on the day James was killed, and she didn't quite know how much about her personal life she wanted to reveal to this man. "Well," she began and was immediately interrupted by her husband.

Mike's voice was steely as he asked, "Why is that important, detective? My wife's feelings about him are irrelevant. She could have loved him or hated him but that doesn't have any bearing on where she was during the crime. Maybe you want to revise your question?"

The young detective was flustered by Mike's interjection, and for a moment, he seemed at a loss as to how he should continue the interview. Finally, he said, "Well, there are quotes from people who were interviewed who said Mrs. Stone had mentioned she'd rather see him dead than married to someone else. I think her feelings might be important."

Mike stood, gave him a long hard stare before he said, "Jana has answered your questions without reservation; there is an entire file documenting an extensive investigation of every link between her and the murder, including suspicions about statements she made and impressions she gave to people. It was determined she was not involved in it; look at the files. It's apparent you have no new evidence or reason to question my wife further. You have begun speculating and you have crossed the line of proper interrogation. So, the interview is over. You may leave now."

Not knowing exactly how he should respond, the young man got up and moved toward the door. Jana rose too and walked with him to the foyer. She placed her hand on his arm as she said, "Forgive my husband, Detective. He is overly protective. To clarify what you may have heard, in the midst of my hurt and anguish over the unexpected divorce, I probably did say I'd rather see him dead than married to someone else, but that was just anger talking. I'm sure you can understand that," she smiled, showing no animosity at all.

Somewhat redeemed by her graciousness, the detective thanked her, and hastily took his leave. When the door closed, Jana went to Mike. "So much for me getting upset," she teased. "Between the two of us, I think I did great, but I can't say the same about you." She put her arms around her husband and gave him a kiss on the cheek. "I love you. You are the best thing that ever happened to me."

Mike hugged her back. Tears stinging his eyes, he said, "Jana, that guy made me so mad. He doesn't know the first thing about conducting an investigation, and for him to ask you that inappropriate question made me want to smack him."

"Forget it," Jana said. "I think you scared him to death. As you told me years ago, there is no evidence pointing to me. We just need to ride this out."

Mike laughed, "So much for me advising you about how to handle this investigation. You did far better than I did."

Later, as Jana thought about the whole incident, she thanked her lucky stars for Mike. He'd helped her so much. She was lucky to have him.

As with many cold cases, the new investigation failed to uncover anything significant enough to warrant continued work. When the newspaper reported the lack of leads and information resulted in tabling the case again, Jana again breathed a sigh of relief. It was comforting to know her secret was still safe.

Chapter 53

The love Jana and Mike had for each other deepened with every passing year. James Browning faded far into the background; he was never mentioned, not because they consciously avoided the subject but because it was something that had no effect on their lives.

Time passed. Weeks turned into months and months turned into years. Although it was hard to realize, their silver anniversary was approaching. Wanting to celebrate their 25 years together in a special way, Jana and Shirley planned a party. Longtime friends came to celebrate with them. A video was shown highlighting their years together. Tears formed in her eyes as Jana watched the special events captured on the clip. The happiness with Mike had filled her life, erasing the bitterness she'd experienced because of her failed first marriage. She never thought about the anguish she'd suffered because of it, or any of the details surrounding it. As she and Mike toasted one another, she was overwhelmed with love and gratitude for her beloved Mike. He was everything to her.

As it always does, the passing of time brought changes. Jana and Mike, like everyone else celebrating decades of birthdays, were presented with unexpected situations that getting older presents. In the beginning, the challenges were easily overcome with minor adjustments. But as time went on, other, more daunting issues couldn't be as easily addressed, and demanded adjustments to their lifestyle.

In the year following their silver wedding anniversary, Jana began experiencing some forgetfulness. At first, it wasn't really a big deal; sometimes she couldn't recall people's names, and other times she'd forget how to make some favorite dish, or she forgot an appointment she'd made. It was aggravating and embarrassing when her mind drew a blank, but mostly she laughed it off, saying old age was catching up with her. Neither she nor Mike paid much attention to the occurrences, but gradually, as they became more pronounced, it wasn't as easy to ignore the lapse in her memory.

The first really alarming incident occurred one night at dinner when she served dessert to Mike. "I made one of your favorites tonight," she said proudly as she brought a big cake with chocolate frosting into the dining room.

"Wow, that looks delicious," Mike said as he eyed the cake with the thick icing.

Jana carefully placed a slice on a saucer and handed it to him. Without hesitation, he took a big bite, expecting to be delighted with the smooth chocolate concoction. But his mouth was filled with a grainy substance; there was nothing sweet at all.

"How is it?" Jana asked expectantly.

"Umm, you taste it," he replied and offered her a big bite on his fork.

"Ugh," she exclaimed as soon as she tasted his offering.

It took several minutes for them to determine that instead of cake flour, cornmeal had been used as an ingredient. Jana was horrified. They decided she'd picked up the wrong canister from the cupboard shelf; the flour and cornmeal sat next to each other.

"I was in a hurry," she said. "I didn't pay attention."

Mike thought it was odd that she hadn't noticed the different color of the substance as she was measuring the amount needed for the cake. And it was perplexing that she hadn't spotted the difference in texture as she blended the ingredients together. But given how upset she was, he didn't comment. He just laughed, making a joke about how the cake wouldn't win any prizes.

They didn't discuss the episode again, but it was the beginning of them eating out more often than having meals at home. If they didn't go out, Mike would go pick up something for them to eat. If Jana did cook, Mike tried to be in the kitchen with her to help prepare the meal. Their once busy kitchen saw less and less activity.

There were other issues as well. The once neat laundry room became a mess. No longer were there orderly stacks of folded items. Things that were dirty were piled on top of those that were clean; there was no telling one from the other. Loads of clean clothes were left in the washer while dried items stayed in the dryer. Mike quietly began handling all laundry chores. Jana seemed not to notice.

He was frustrated to have their once orderly life in such chaos, but Mike managed to overcome the challenges by not having Jana in charge of daily activities. He was, however, aware that the situation was getting harder to handle, and almost impossible to overlook.

Chapter 54

Mike was home one Tuesday afternoon waiting for Jana to get home from her weekly hair appointment when the telephone rang. "Mr. Stone?" the voice asked when he answered the call.

"Yes, this is Mike Stone," he replied cautiously, not recognizing the voice.

"I'm patrolman Bennett, with the State Highway Department, and I'm here on Ashley Boulevard with your wife, Jana," the caller explained.

"Is she all right? Has there been an accident?" Mike asked anxiously.

The patrolman, responding quietly but firmly, said, "There hasn't been an accident, but you need to come get your wife. I saw her on the side of the road, standing beside her automobile, obviously distressed, and I stopped to see if she needed assistance. She's very confused, and unsure of how to get home. I got your number from the emergency contact card in her wallet. She's in no condition to drive."

After asking their neighbor, Charles, to go with him, Mike set out to get Jana. His thoughts went over the other incidents when Jana hadn't been able to recall simple information. He admitted that lately she'd been confused a great deal of the time, not seeming to be able to function. He said to the neighbor, "I don't understand what's going on with her; she keeps forgetting things and she's confused most of the time."

Charles looked at him for a moment and then replied, "There has been a change in her over the last few months. We've noticed several things that didn't make sense and wanted to talk to you about it but weren't quite sure how to broach the subject. There seems to be something major happening to her; she's definitely not herself."

Hearing Charles confirm what he and his wife had been noticing was like a punch in the stomach. Although he had been very uneasy about her for a while, for the first time, he was struck by the stark reality that there were major problems with Jana, in spite of the excuses he manufactured for the things that concerned him. Before he could respond, Charles pointed to the side of the road where Jana was standing beside a uniformed patrolman.

Quickly pulling over and stopping, Mike got out of the car and headed straight toward her. Looking up, she spotted him and ran as fast as she could, arms extended toward him with tears streaming down her face. Her words were gut wrenching. "I don't know where I am or how I got here," she said brokenly. "Please take me home."

Gently hugging her and murmuring that everything was all right, he got her settled in his car. He spoke briefly with the patrolman who emphasized Jana hadn't broken any laws but given her confusion he couldn't let her drive. Before leaving, he advised Mike that she shouldn't be driving at all. After Charles left in Jana's car, Mike walked slowly back to his, not at all sure how he was going to handle Jana's reaction to the whole situation. But strangely enough, she didn't have anything to say. She sobbed most of the way home, in spite of his reassurances that everything was okay. At one point she stared at him pitifully, asking, "What's happening to me, Mike? I'm not able to do anything anymore."

Hearing her admission, Mike felt tears welling in his eyes. It was, indeed, the turning point, calling for action. Mike insisted Jana go to their family physician, who listened to Mike's description of Jana's issues, as well as questioning Jana. He determined a routine physical was in order and when it was completed, said they'd be contacted when the lab work results were received.

The lab tests were normal, and the doctor ordered more extensive medical tests. After a month filled with X-Rays, CAT scans, MRI's, plus two psychological evaluations, Jana and Mike were summoned back to meet with the physician to discuss the results.

The doctor began by delivering good news that the tests had shown Jana was in excellent physical condition with no indication of a tumor or heart irregularity. Then looking directly at Mike, he spoke very quietly, saying, "Given the results of the tests along with the symptoms she is experiencing, the conclusion is that this is the onset of dementia."

"I know some things about dementia, but what exactly does it mean for Jana?" Mike asked glancing quickly in her direction.

"Well, some people think it's a condition due to the aging process, but dementia symptoms typically develop slowly and may only become noticeable when memory lapses become more of a disruption to daily routines," the doctor replied. "At this point there's no way of knowing how fast it will progress or how severe it will be. Unfortunately, there is no cure although certain medications can be prescribed that seem to slow the progress. Like most medicines, there are some side effects."

Furtively, Mike shot a quick look at Jana, who appeared to be uninterested in the conversation; her focus was on the framed photographs hanging on the wall behind the doctor's desk. "What treatment is there to deter it?" Mike questioned.

"To better explain how it manifests itself and what steps are beneficial, I want you to have these pamphlets," he said, pulling a stack of booklets from his desk and handing them to Mike. "You should read them carefully, learn all you can and implement as many of the suggestions for dealing with Jana as possible. If after you weigh the pros and cons and decide to give her medication, I'll prescribe it for her. We can start with the mildest and work from there."

Mike stared at him blankly, unable to fully absorb what he'd just heard. His voice very quiet, the doctor's words were heartfelt, "I'm sorry, Mike. I wish there were some physical problem that could be solved, but that doesn't appear to be the case. If you have further questions or if you become concerned about Jana, call the office and I'll be glad to see her."

As they stood to leave Jana asked, "Well, do I have to take any medicine?"

"No, the tests indicated you don't need to be medicated. You are in great physical shape; you just take care of yourself," the doctor replied.

Reverting to her no-nonsense personality, she declared, "Well, all this was certainly a waste of time and money, wasn't it?"

Remembering the direct, say-what-you-mean Jana, the doctor chuckled as he patted her on the back and shook Mike's hand.

Chapter 55

The next weeks were very unsettling for Mike. On one hand, he wanted to ignore Jana's diagnosis and continue making excuses for her behavior. But, on the other hand, there were too many indications that her dementia was progressing at a rapid pace. Usually very social, she lost interest in attending events or gatherings, preferring to stay at home. All meal preparation ceased; in fact, unless Mike brought it to her attention, eating did not seem to cross her mind.

Upkeep of their house became a problem. Jana no longer did any of the chores required to keep things in order and she would not tolerate the maid service Mike hired. After much agonizing, Mike decided it was time to move to an assisted living facility. Jana resisted the idea at first, but after a while, it wasn't discussed any more. When the move finally occurred, she seemed not to notice her new surroundings. Mike was heartbroken over leaving their home, but he was determined to do what was best for her.

During the next year, Jana's ability to function became more and more limited. Her conversations seldom made sense. Mostly, they involved something from the past; it was very rare when she was concerned about current things. One morning when they were sitting at the breakfast table, she announced, "I'm going to Grafton's end-of-season sale today. I'm sure they will have some really good items."

Mike looked at her for a moment and then nodded, without speaking. He didn't want a confrontation with her, and it would do no good to tell her that Grafton's department store had been closed for over a decade. The best thing to do was to say nothing; chances were good she'd forget she'd mentioned going there. Not seeming to notice that he didn't reply, she began talking in detail about the store's dressing rooms. "I use the ones at the back of the store," she said. "They are never as crowded; you have more privacy there. No one pays any attention to who goes in or out. I have some things on hold there; I need to get them," she said firmly.

"Okay, we'll go later this afternoon," Mike said. "Why don't you make a list of the things you want to check out."

Hearing his words, a bright smile wreathed Jana's face and she began moving toward the door. As she left the room, Mike sighed. It was so sad to see her living in the past. The things she came up with were astounding. He thought about how, for some unknown reason, she'd become obsessed with s'mores, the treat kids often made at outdoor gatherings. Over and over, she talked about roasting marshmallows, saying the fire needed to burn down so that the embers would be just right for making them. Mike couldn't recall their ever having eaten s'mores; most certainly they'd never made them. But to hear Jana, you'd think they were a mainstay in their house.

When he asked the doctor why she was talking about something totally unrelated to their life, Dr. Abbott carefully explained it was probably something Jana had done when she was a kid; he said many dementia patients remembered things from long ago. He also said the patients confused actual events with things they'd seen on television or read about in the past, stressing that many of the stories were fabrications and should not be taken as fact.

"You just have to realize her life is a combination of memory and fantasy," he'd said. "We are part of everything we do, places we visit, people we meet, books we've read and movies and television shows we've seen and all of that is part of the dementia patient's life. They can't always separate actual events from reality."

Hearing the doctor's explanation made some sense to Mike, especially when he considered Jana's stories about the lake. Although he knew that during her first marriage, much time had been spent boating, it was not a past time he and Jana enjoyed and, except for a few rare occasions, they'd never been on the lake. But suddenly she'd began talking about how much she loved boating, saying being on the water was her favorite past-time, describing in great detail how pretty the view was from some high bridge. She recalled picnics, and trips there that, as far as Mike knew, were all a fantasy. She spoke endlessly about taking flowers to toss on the water.

And while she would talk about things that never happened, surprisingly, sometimes her stories did have a factual basis. Mike recognized that the tales she told about Shirley, her good friend, did have a measure of validity. She loved telling about how she and Shirley took a self-defense course together and how they'd both bought guns. Mike knew that was true; it was one of the first things he'd learned while investigating the murder of Jana's ex-husband. She took such great delight in recounting those escapades, saying she was far better marksman than Shirley. She always ended them by laughing and slapping her knee, declaring, "Shirley never knew how I fooled her!" The saddest part of her memories of Shirley was that she didn't remember that Shirley had died fifteen years before. She spoke of her as if she were living and that they still saw one another.

Another oddity was how she loved having fresh roses in their apartment, declaring they were her favorite flower. After she and Mike married, they never had them in their home. That she suddenly wanted roses around her could have been that she was remembering the rose garden she used to have Mike supposed. It really didn't make sense, but he dutifully brought her a bouquet of them once a week.

Dealing with the transformed Jana was difficult for Mike, but his love for her mandated commitment to her care. Heeding the advice of her physician, he didn't contradict or interrupt her long dissertations and he didn't correct her; he just tolerated her rambling. He just let her talk since it seemed to make her happy. As time went on, he rarely ever really paid attention when she began one of her stories but there were instances when he had to intervene.

One morning he found her rummaging in their closet and asked, "What are you looking for?"

"Those canvas flats, the ones that are too big for me; you know, I stuffed tissue paper in the toes to make them fit properly," she answered in frustration as she frantically shoved the things around on the closet floor.

Mike looked at her quizzically, not having a clue about any shoes she'd stuffed with tissue paper. "They will show up," he said in an effort to appease her. "I'm sure you put them somewhere."

The look she gave him was scathing. "You don't understand; I need to take them to that big donation box at the shopping center. I have to get rid of them."

"Well it won't matter when you take them; don't waste your time looking for something you don't need," he said in a soothing tone. "Why don't we go over to the activity center and see what's going on?" he continued in an effort to divert her attention.

Immediately her attitude changed, and she replied, "Okay, that's a good idea," already forgetting about the shoes. Mike shook his head as she got up from the floor of the closet and went out the door.

Chapter 56

As dementia claimed her, Mike became resigned to the fact that the Jana he had known and loved for so long was gone. He never knew what new challenges he would encounter as the result of her progressing condition. Trying to keep the person she'd become calm and happy, he was often frustrated and unsure of how he should handle her ever-evolving personality.

He missed his Jana. Sometimes, when he looked up and saw her across the room, he would be taken back in time and, for a moment, she would be the dear person he'd loved for so many years. Then, in a flash, hearing some senseless remark from her, the reality that what he was seeing was only an outward copy of his precious Jana became evident. The times when she demanded he do something outlandish would remind him that his precious wife was gone forever, that what was left was just an empty shell. He tried to accommodate her new likes and dislikes, accepting the changes dementia had wrought on her; but, as time went on, it became more difficult.

One of the strangest issues surfaced when Jana became enamored with the church that began providing worship services at the Assisted Living facility. She and Mike were not members of any church; they'd never attended worship services, and, except for a beautiful leather edition which was on the coffee table in the living room, there wasn't a Bible in their home. Mike's participation in religious activities had ceased when he left home for college. Through his growing up years, his parents had insisted he attend church, but once he was on his own, he chose not to continue the practice. Organized religion held no attraction to him. And, as far as he knew, Jana had never participated in church activities. She celebrated Christmas and Easter, but they were centered on Santa

Claus and the Easter Bunny, not anything religious. He did not object when Jana told him she wanted to go to church. He'd been sure her interest would wane as it had with all activities provided by the facility. But from the first time she went to a service, she was completely fascinated with every aspect of it.

Mike tried accompanying her, but the services were very different from the conservative ones he'd grown up attending, and he did not care for them. In his opinion, the loud guitar music and hand clapping that dominated them was more entertainment than worship. After a couple of attempts, in spite of wanting to be with Jana, he decided it was too much for him. She, on the other hand, was quite taken with the whole scenario. So, three times a week he walked with her to the activity center where the service was held, and then he went to the adjoining library until it was over.

Before long, Jana's conversations were centered on seeking forgiveness, and loving your fellow man. She often talked about confessing her secret sins, and without fail, she'd become very upset, and almost frantic. It didn't take long when she started down that path for Mike to become proficient at quickly changing the subject, intervening with some diversion to change her focus.

As Jana's condition steadfastly deteriorated Mike made some decisions safeguarding her future. Ten years older than her, he was well aware that the possibility she would outlive him needed to be addressed. Having no children or close relatives, it was up to him to be sure Jana was properly cared for in the event he preceded her in death. Meetings with both their attorney and the Assisted Living facility's administrators culminated in detailed arrangements being put in place in the event of his death, to transfer her to the nursing home which was part of the retirement community. Having that settled gave him peace of mind.

It was a testimony to the love he had for her. She was so very special. Their years together had been a blessing; he was grateful for the life they'd shared. He treasured the memories of the Jana that had been his wife, and he wanted the best care for her always.

PART FOUR

Chapter 57

It was after midnight, and except for an occasional cough, or moan, the nursing home was quiet. Hallway lights were dimmed because doors to the resident's rooms remained open for monitoring purposes. Having finished their hourly bed checks, Pam and Chelsea, assigned to wing 4 were at the nurse's station. While Pam updated patient charts, Chelsea assembled medication for the morning rounds. When a light on the call board lit up, Chelsea noted who had called for assistance, smiled, quickly rose from her chair, locked the medicine cabinet, dropped the keys in her pocket and said, "I'll go."

Chelsea really liked Mrs. Stone. Although eighty-seven years old, she still had the remnants of beauty from her youth. She loved having her hair done and her nails painted almost as much as she loved talking to people. It was unusual for her to need assistance at such a late hour.

"What's the matter Mrs. Stone?" Chelsea asked as she entered her room and turned the call button to 'off.'

"I can't sleep," the elderly woman said fretfully.

"What's bothering you, dear?" Chelsea asked kindly.

"I did a terrible thing many years ago," she said, "I can't quit thinking about it."

Chelsea nodded her head thoughtfully, thinking how sad it was for Mrs. Stone to be wrestling with something that had probably never occurred. All the residents on wing 4 had dementia, in her case Alzheimer's. Chelsea's training taught her to deal with kindness and compassion when she worked with patients suffering from those conditions. She was well acquainted with how their minds wandered from reality to fantasy. It was such a shame to see once vibrant people sink into oblivion, not knowing who they were or why they had to leave their homes. Entire families suffered when those decisions had to be made. She felt so sorry for the relatives and friends who had to deal with loved ones who no longer knew them. It was heartbreaking to watch as they tried to capture some small assurance, they were recognized by those who'd been a part of their life for years and were now immersed in the depths of a condition not understood by anyone.

Even more disturbing were the residents who had no one who cared or visited them. That was the case with Mrs. Stone. She was all alone, with no family or friends to visit her. Chelsea had learned that after Mrs. Stone's husband died, according to his instructions, she'd been moved from the assisted-living apartment complex where they'd lived, to the nursing home.

Mrs. Stone loved to talk; she told such wild stories, repeating the same ones over and over. She might have an occasional moment of clarity when she'd asked a meaningful question or made an appropriate comment about something; however, for the most part, she would begin talking about one thing and end her recitation by switching subjects entirely, making no sense at all. Mostly she talked about her husband, sometimes calling him Mike and other times referring to him as James. Her favorite questions were "What day is this?" and "What am I supposed to do now?" She was always talking about taking it easy which Chelsea assumed was what her husband had said to her when she became upset. She talked incessantly about love and forgiveness and the importance of confessing sins. Chelsea assumed religion had been a major part of her life until dementia took over. No one paid attention to her ramblings, but she was such a gentle soul. Chelsea listened to her whenever time permitted. Witnessing her escalating confusion really tugged at Chelsea's heartstrings. Seeing the sweet lady in such a state prompted Chelsea's attempt to ease her anxiety by quietly reassuring her that everything was all right, and that she should indeed take it easy.

"Let me get you a drink of water and then you can tell me all about what's bothering you," Chelsea said soothingly as she straightened the covers on Mrs. Stone's bed.

"It's time for me to confess!" Mrs. Stone was clearly agitated. "I've tried before, but no one pays attention. I've kept it secret all these years, but I need to be forgiven."

"Well why don't you have a drink of water, and then you can tell me your secret," Chelsea said. "I promise I will listen."

After the old woman finished drinking, Chelsea pulled a chair over to her bedside. "Now, what's this secret you need to confess?" she asked, gently taking one of the old lady's hands in hers. She fully expected that Mrs. Stone wouldn't remember what she'd been talking about and was a bit surprised when she immediately began speaking.

"You see, no one ever knew what I did. I planned it all by myself and I kept it from everyone."

Chelsea murmured softly, "It's all right, dear. Whatever it was, isn't important. Just close your eyes and get some rest."

"I can't rest. I need to confess. I need forgiveness!" The old woman was getting more and more agitated.

Realizing she needed to be placated, Chelsea sighed and said, "You can tell me your secret. I'm sure you will be forgiven."

"Well you see, I wasn't always married to Mike," Mrs. Stone began, continuing her sentence saying, "he came along afterward. He didn't have anything to do with the original events."

Her rambling made no sense. It was the same old things she always talked about, how taking it easy was an important part of her life and how hard she'd worked to be successful at it. Chelsea, tired from a very long day, let her mind wander. Thinking it probably wouldn't be long until the elderly woman fell asleep, Chelsea thought she'd just relax and take a breather while the elderly woman rambled on.

The old woman continued her saga by talking about how happy she was on her wedding day. Chelsea smiled, thinking it must have been at least forty years since she and Mr. Stone married. She hoped she would be able to recall her wedding day with such fondness after that many years passed. When Mrs. Stone closed her eyes, Chelsea was sure she'd be asleep in a minute, but to her surprise Mrs. Stone began talking again.

"Although I thought I'd come to grips with the situation, seeing him at the wedding made me realize he would always be just around the corner, taunting me whenever he could. I realized there was no way for me to move on if I had to see him all the time, especially if he was with her."

It was a peculiar statement, and Chelsea looked at Mrs. Stone in surprise waiting for her to continue. But, as always, the woman's mind drifted and she began talking about making detailed plans, and rehearsing speeches to answer questions. It was her usual pattern of jumping from one subject to another, none of it making sense. As the ramblings continued, Chelsea found her mind wandering. It wasn't until she heard the old woman say something about getting the gun from the cabinet that Chelsea started paying attention.

And what she heard was riveting. Jana Stone relayed a story so fascinating and detail oriented that Chelsea was amazed. *Wow,* she thought as she listened to the woman. *What a tale! She must have watched hundreds of television shows to come up with something like that!*

Mrs. Stone continued in a soft, low voice, "There were times when I wanted to tell Mike everything, but he would have been so hurt. I just couldn't do that to him. He thought I was something special. But he's gone now; and it won't be long until I'm gone too. I've realized what I did was a sin and I'm confessing and asking for forgiveness. I'm truly sorry."

Chelsea patted the old woman's hand and murmured softly, "You're forgiven Mrs. Stone. You can quit worrying about it." Almost magically, after hearing that declaration, the old woman relaxed. A look of peace fell over her and she closed her eyes and drifted off to sleep.

Chelsea tucked the blanket around the frail body, clipped the call button where she could reach it and made her way out of the room, her mind wondering about the tale she'd just heard. The thought that she'd look through Mrs. Stone's file and see her history crossed her mind, but as she entered the hall, an emergency alert sounded. The man in the room at the end of the corridor was in distress. Hurrying toward his room, she put Mrs. Stone's story out of her mind.

It was an hour later before things settled down, and Chelsea and the other staff had to work furiously to get everything ready for the morning shift. Finally leaving at 7:00 a.m., she was exhausted, more than ready to enjoy the next two days when she wasn't scheduled to work.

Returning to work on Friday, during the morning resident update session, she was saddened to hear that Mrs. Stone had passed away. The Nursing Supervisor said she never woke up after Chelsea left her Tuesday night; she'd died in her sleep.

Thank you for reading my book.

If you want to let me know what you think about it, I would love to hear from you at

patjacksonbooks@gmail.com

Made in the USA
Monee, IL
12 July 2020